MUSCLE MEN

MUSCLE MEN

ROCK-HARD GAY EROTICA

Edited by
Richard Labonté

CLEIS
PRESS

Published in the United States by Cleis Press Inc., 2246 Sixth Street, Berkeley, California 94710.

Printed in the United States.
Cover design: Scott Idleman
Cover photo: altrendo images
Text design: Frank Wiedemann
Cleis Press logo art: Juana Alicia
First Edition.
10 9 8 7 6 5 4 3 2 1

ISBN: 978-1-57344-392-0

"Brute" © 2010 by Jonathan Asche. "Mr. Muscle Pump" © 2010 by Steven Bereznai. "The Gimp, the Vig and the Ring" © 2010 by Michael Bracken. "Bigchest: Confessions of a Tit Man" © 2010 by Larry Duplechan. "The Ambivalent Gardener and the State of Grace" © 2010 by Jamie Freeman. "Muscle Worship: If I Said You Have a Beautiful Body, Would You Hold It Against Me?" © 2010 by Jack Fritscher, appeared in different versions in *Skin* (January 1981), *Inches* (March 1987), *Drummer* (December 1988), and *Some Dance to Remember: A Memoir-Novel of San Francisco 1970-1982* (© 1990, 2005), reprinted with the author's permission. "Bobby Lo versus the Evil Sakata" © 2010 by Thomas Fuchs. "Muscle Meeting" © 2010 by Jeff Jacklin. "Fight Cub" © 2010 by Geoffrey Knight. "After Hours" © 2010 by Dale Lazarov and Bastian Jonsson. "The Lair of Carlo de la Paz" © 2009 by Joe Marohl, reprinted with the author's permission from velvetmafia.com. "Details" © 2010 by Natty Soltesz. "Thunder and Lightning" © 2010 by Cage Thunder. "Nephilim Lover" © 2010 by Rob Wolfsham.

For Asa.
Again.
He keeps getting it right.

Contents

INTRODUCTION: FOR ME IT'S THE FOREARM

For some gay men, it's all about muscle: sleek muscle, bulging muscle, muscle to stroke lightly, muscle to squeeze hard, muscle to punch until it reddens and swells, muscle to wrestle on the mat until it's sheathed with sweat, muscle to cum on, muscle to cuddle. It's about certain muscles: bouncing pecs or rounded biceps or boulder shoulders or steely traps or flared backs or solid butts or thick thighs or sculpted calves. It's about unrequited lust or a distant gaze or the stored fantasy of muscle worship.

For me, it's only about forearms.

I'm not sure why I'm most stirred by a meaty forearm. Was it the sight in boyhood of an auto mechanic wrenching with all his might against a recalcitrant tire lug? The flex of an older boy's arm next to me as he pulled open a stubborn high school locker door? The muscular wrist-to-elbow ripple of the kid climbing rope ahead of me in gym?

But there you are: taste just is.

The body beefy or the body ripped certainly can appeal, as the stories in this collection about men and muscles attest.

Reading the dozens of submissions was great fun, often a turn-on for me, as well-written prose with a porn focus can be. But, in the end, the submissions were disappointing: not a single writer focused on the glory of a striated forearm, a forearm as thick as most men's upper arms, a forearm built for wrestling other men's mighty arms to the table. Sigh. Not even a busy editor of eclectic erotica always gets what he wants....

But that's just me. The rest of you have a smorgasbord of muscle, from martial art prowess to bodybuilding subservience, from wrestling dominance to boxing lust, from muscled fighters to muscled lovers, from intense muscle worship to fleeting muscle encounters. And though reading about muscle is exciting, looking at is always a thrill—so I've included two muscle comics. You may touch the pages if you wish.

In erotic writing, the line between fact and fantasy, between memory and imagination, is often mutable. For some contributors, "write what you know" is a mantra. For others, the story is wrought from an inventive mind rather than a physical experience. Both types of tales are included in *Muscle Men*. But I've closed with a piece that's a balls-out essay—nothing unreal about it. Larry Duplechan's coda isn't muscle fiction; it's muscle fact, a reflection on his hormone-fueled boyhood attraction to—and desire to become—what many gay men fantasize about: muscle. And if you want to eroticize the writer rather than, as is usually the case, the writing, you have my permission. Larry's, too.

Richard Labonté
Bowen Island, British Columbia

THE LAIR OF CARLO DE LA PAZ

Joe Marohl

Carlo is seventy-two. He comes to the club on Wednesdays, chats up a couple of boys he finds interesting, invites them to his place to fight each other. In his basement he's set up a twenty-by-twenty pro-wrestling ring, with canvas mat and vinyl-padded turnbuckles. Carlo never enters the match. He sits in the shadows and smokes Tareytons. He doesn't video the match, he doesn't cheer the fighters on, he doesn't request particular holds or moves or punches. On the whole he seems to favor actual fighting, but he doesn't complain when two guys simply pose and flex in skimpy trunks and clown around. At the end of the evening he pays each guy 25 twenty-dollar bills wrapped in a pink rubber band.

I know these details because some of these same guys come home with me from time to time, to fuck or to fight or to fuck and fight, and they tell me things. The guys tend to be young, with slim waists and tight, defined muscle.

Tonight Carlo is talking with someone a bit older. This guy

looks like he's in his midthirties: tan, solid, five ten or five eleven, with a jawline that throbs as he grinds his teeth and, when he uses it, a bright generous smile. Dark chest hair peeks out at the collar of his V-neck tee, and his arms are sinewy and covered with hair. Carlo buys the man a drink—a whiskey, neat. He laughs at something the guy says. From where I sit, the man looks incredibly handsome: masculine, unaffected, comfortable in his skin.

Then, unexpectedly, Carlo makes eye contact with me. He smiles, tips his glass to me. I'm forty-five in two months, sturdy and rectangular, with a start-up spare tire round my waist, not at all Carlo's usual type. He signals for me to join them. As far as I know, Carlo doesn't know me from Adam, but as I approach, he calls me by name—let's say it *is* Adam—and introduces me to Robert.

With an ease that belies the oddness of his request, he asks Robert and me if we'd be interested in beating each other up. "Why not?" we answer, smiling with our teeth, locking eyes and nervously downing the rest of our drinks.

Everything at Carlo's place is pretty much as I imagined it. Under his piss-elegant manse, furnished in Italian and Chinese antiques, with the odd Mbunda mask thrown in as punctuation, a carpeted stairwell leads to the fight lair, the ring garishly lit with bright spots and the whitewashed cinder-block walls decorated with boxing and pro-wrestling posters from the Eisenhower years.

Robert and I strip and slip on the boots and old-fashioned knit trunks Carlo hands us—Robert in baby blue, me in cocoa brown. We climb into the ring, test the ropes, look into the lights sheepishly, then back into opposite corners. Carlo sits nearby on an overstuffed leather chair, legs crossed at the knees, Tareyton in hand.

I spread my arms, gripping the top ring rope, and size up my opponent. Robert is muscular, a blanket of hair across his chest that tapers attractively down to his navel. His legs too are hairy, proportionate to his strong torso, with striated thighs and dense, rock-hard calves. I bend at the waist, stretching to loosen up and make myself relax. I'm taller by an inch or so. My muscle is bigger but not so well defined. I've got more profuse and more unruly body hair. I'd say our butch factors are evenly matched, but Robert's visible toughness intimidates me, especially now that he's no longer smiling.

The start-up bell sounds. I shake myself loose of the turn-buckle and bounce toward the center of the ring, rolling my shoulders. Robert charges straight at me, brows down, eyes blazing. He slugs me cross the mouth with a hard right, then jabs me in the gut with his left. I fold in half. Robert wedges my head between his arm and rib cage and flips me over his shoulders. My back crashes to the canvas. Okay, so we're not going to clown around.

Robert backs off, bouncing from one foot to the other, his pecs loosely flexing, his fists poised right over his belly.

I roll over and jump back up on my feet, no sooner done than Robert is right there at me. He slaps me cross the face and shoves me back to the turnbuckle, drives his knee to my abs, three times. The guy's face is serious as a car bomb. He clenches his forearms at the back of my skull and smashes my face to his chest.

My hands grope at his shoulders. I throw blind punches to his lats. Finally I get my hands up at his face, jam them hard against his mouth and nostrils and manage to push my way out of the corner and shove him to the ring ropes. I punish his inner thigh with my knee, to tenderize the muscle. My whole weight presses his body to the ropes, while his chest hair burns my face.

Under the lights our bodies glisten with sweat. Our groans and the sounds of flesh smacking flesh echo cross the cinderblock walls.

I manage to thrust myself loose of him. His eyes bore into mine, his face frozen in a determined grimace. He attacks me with a pair of roundhouse punches at the center of the ring. I fire back to the chin, and he drops to one knee. I grab his ears and ram my kneecap to his lips. The knee comes back bloody, and Robert collapses on his side, stars and spirals spinning over his head.

I back away, see his shining belly contract and expand. His diaphragm quivers. One of his knees arches unsteadily toward the spotlights.

I look over at Carlo. The man is motionless, silent, without expression in the dark.

I climb up to the top rung of the turnbuckle, something I always wanted to try out. I leap and land on Robert's torso like a waffle iron. He grunts. His body thrashes. My chest bearing down hard on his, I grab his raised knee and pull it up to my armpit. With my free arm I pound on the canvas...one...two... but Robert powers out of the pin, pushes me off, and backhands me cross the jaw.

We get up on our knees, knee to knee, and slug it out. The glint in Robert's eye tells me he's liking this—punching no more nor less than getting punched. My cock stiffens. We exhaust ourselves, and in a matter of a minute we are propping our bodies against each other. Carlo intervenes. He rings the bell and orders us back to our corners. He tosses us each a towel to wipe ourselves down.

I fix my eyes on Robert at the opposite corner. Like mine, his towel is pink with blood. His glistening skin is spotted with flecks of dirt off the canvas. He breathes deeply in and out. His eyes return my gaze. He nods respectfully, but with a hard glaze over his expression that means he won't give an inch.

Carlo lets us cool down. After ten minutes, the bell rings for round two.

The blood pounds in my veins. Robert and I meet in the center and lock hands, my right and his left. The spotlights burn down on our shoulders. We test our strength, push, pull, twist, squeeze. Then we lock our free hands together, stretch our arms wide, bump chests and bellies, breathe through our teeth.

Robert bends my arms, forcing me back three or four steps. I anchor my left heel to the canvas and stand firm, manage to push my arms back to an even position.

We break and circle each other. I reach over and slap Robert on the side of his head. He reciprocates. We lock arms and shove our shoulders together. Our heads and necks brace each other. Robert's hot breath bathes my strained trapezoid muscle. Our boots kick against each other's legs, a kind of dance testing for weakness and angling for dominance.

Robert hooks his leg to my left knee and knocks me off balance. I roll on my back, and he spins into a leg lock and falls on his butt. Pain explodes up from my knee to the sides of my head. I try to drive my right leg to his face, but he intercepts it and forces it to the mat.

It's a classic figure-four submission hold, but I don't give in. Instead I savor the pain, silently pray it toughens me. Robert smiles. He stretches back to add pressure to my joints. The agony is exquisite, like lightning surging through my veins, my bones crumpling like breadsticks, or so it seems. I drum my elbows against the canvas, my throat too tight to scream. Robert rocks us back and forth, to pound in the last ounce of hurt.

My skin goes clammy, my legs numb. My temples throb. My dick stiffens in the knitted trunks, pushing upward to the elastic waistband. Blindly I stretch out, feel the bottom ring rope against my knuckles, and manage to grip it. Robert breaks the hold and backs up to his corner.

The hold released, I feel a new wave of pain, almost as if the pressure of the hold had somehow been blocking part of the hurt below my knees. I hold on to the ring rope like a lifeline. I pull myself up to it, thrust my shoulder over it, inhale and exhale in deep gasps, greedy for oxygen. My whole body tingles.

Robert approaches. At first he hovers, his eyes examining every detail of my helplessness. Then he grabs my boots and tries to pull me clear of the ropes. I hold on. He straddles my back and begins clawing at my fingers.

"Let go," he growls. "Time to do this."

My grip weakens. Robert drives his leg to my ribs—five times. I pull my knees to my chest and roll over on my back. Robert stands and leans down, slapping and punching my arms and head. I drive my heel straight to his 'nads. He howls and stumbles backward, bent over.

Reluctant to let go of the ropes, I stare at him for several seconds. Then I pull myself to my feet. I charge at him and kick him in the face. He flies back and crashes to the canvas. I kneel on his chest, grab his curly black hair in my left fist, and start pummeling his face with my right.

The bell sounds. Heedlessly, I sneak in two more punches before retreating to my corner.

Slowly, Robert rolls over on his side, crawls to the ring ropes to pull himself up and parks his butt against the opposite turn-buckle. He looks up at me. His face is meat, his gaze stiletto sharp.

Carlo tosses us clean towels. The sweat and blood on my skin are now like grease. I rub the towel over my face, neck, chest, stomach, between my thighs. I let the scuzzy rag drop to the ground. My cock presses hard against the brown trunks, all the more so when I catch a good look at Robert's hard-on.

Robert pinches his pecs to massage them. He rubs the flat of his hand across his abs. He back-kicks the turnbuckle, impatient.

Round three: the bell no sooner sounds than Robert shouts, "Payback time, Adam."

He thrusts his leg out from the waist, karate style, and smashes my groin. The blow knocks me off my feet and flat on my back. Feels like I've got a wasp nest in my trunks.

Robert grabs me by the ears and pulls my head up, making sure my face brushes up the full length of his leg, over the firm bulge of his shaft, slides up the skin of his belly, the thick hair of his chest, till he's looking me square in the eye, not six inches away. He spits in my mouth, then butts his forehead to mine.

I see and hear all this more vividly than I feel it. The head butt echoes emptily in my skull. Robert's eyes are dead—bright but humorless. My body feels like a sack of shit. Everything's like it's underwater.

Robert grinds my face to the top ring rope, sliding my nose and lips a good four feet over the taut vinyl. I turn, my arms stretched out on the rope. Robert drives his knee to my chest, then thrashes my mouth with his forearm. I clasp the rope. He pulls me up by my boots and yanks me to the center of the ring, my shoulder blades smashing the canvas.

Groggily I open my eyes. Robert drives his knee to the back of my left thigh, then rests his right knee on my other thigh. His blue trunks clearly outline the engorged lump underneath. The tip, in fact, is nearly visible at his waistband, a bead of precum dampening the skin under his belly button.

He grabs my legs again and flips me over on my belly. My knees in his armpits, he drops his butt on my lower back. I pound the canvas with my hands and howl, tears streaking my face. He leans back, stretching my stomach and twisting my spine. His cock nudges the top of my ass. I stretch my arms to grab the ring rope, but it's nearly a foot out of reach.

I start to tap out, but he leans back farther. My tendons feel like they're snapping now. I reach behind me and manage to grab a fistful of his hair and yank with everything I've got, pulling his head to the mat and forcing him to release one of my legs. I catch his neck in the crook of my right arm and choke him. He loses the hold on my other leg, and I pull up to him.

I try to rise up to my feet, but he grabs the bottom of my trunks and tugs them down. The elastic snags on my hard dick, but I know I'm showing crack and pubes right now. I kick his lower abdomen with my knee. Our bodies collapse together side by side, our skin slippery and steaming hot under the lights, our muscles rubbery with fatigue but engorged by the action.

I crawl on his back like it's a surfboard, my chest on his shoulder blades, my stiffy nestled teasingly between his firm, round cheeks. I brace my forearm between the bridge of his nose and his upper lip and jerk the back of his head to my throat. I wrench his head backward. He pounds the canvas with his hands and feet. I pound my hips to his butt, to hurt and to humiliate. His bucking only makes me harder.

"I give," he groans. "Stop. Please. I submit."

I let his head go. His forehead falls to his forearm. I ruffle his hair with my fingers.

Robert's back heaves as he catches his breath. I grab the waistband of his blue trunks and pull them down off his muscular glutes, down his hard furry thighs, and let them rest below his knees. Robert keeps his face down to the mat and doesn't move. I push my trunks down to my knees. Robert spreads his legs and raises his butt.

I dip into him, our bodies still slick and hot from the fight. Christ, he feels nice inside: ass hairs drenched in sweat, smooth interior muscle coiling against the tender veins of my cock.I push and push, skin soughing on skin. He moans, reaches down and strokes his own cock, which is now glued to his stomach.

I pull out and rest my cock against his lower spine. I caress his head and pull it, gently now, to my chest. We roll on our sides. Robert shoots first, spattering cum up to the top of his hairy chest. I slide my shaft on his glistening skin. The inside of my skin seems to glow. I sense the vague dizziness of climax approach, and I shoot up to his shoulder blades.

We lie side by side, not speaking.

I look up and see that Carlo has left the lair. On the leather cushion where he sat lie two green rolls of cash. My arms embrace Robert from behind, my forearms locked across his chest. My nose finds a place to settle between his ear and his dark curly hair. I whisper, "Can we do this again?"

He whispers, "Rematch, bossman. Definitely."

MR. MUSCLE PUMP

Steven Bereznai

There's the crackle of fluorescent lights, a clank of weights and grunts of pain. The pungent smell of bronzer, sweat and baby oil mix in the air, making the place smell like a locker room tanning salon. But only the best of the best, the hottest of the hottest, the most muscular of the muscular have made it to this elite venue: it's backstage at the Mr. Muscle Pump Championships.

The finest corn-fed boys from across the Midwest have been building their physiques for this one moment, a chance to show off their bods before a crowd of worshipping fans and merciless judges, waiting to see them strut, flex and pose.

Strict dieting and torturous workouts have gotten them this far, along with brutal waxing sessions that have left them looking like silky smooth muscle pops. Now it's time for the finishing touches before the men take the stage.

Some of the competitors wear tank tops, their pecs and nipples toppling out of peekaboo spaghetti straps, but most are stripped down to skimpy posing trunks that are as close to naked as the rules allow. There's plenty to look at: delts, quads, glutes and biceps, ripped and buffed from hours in the gym and a few steroids thrown in for good measure. The guys check each other out, sizing up the competition.

Amidst the slabs of muscle, Rodney Jarrod stands out. His nickname's "the Rod," a name he more than lives up to. Rumor is he earned it back in military college. He got booted out for cracking heads with his pistol. The story's true, more or less, but one glance at the massive mound in his crotch and it's clear what weapon he was using—and it wasn't skulls he was busting open.

His rugged face is ugly handsome, with a high forehead, a crooked nose and a chin you could break a chisel on. It's the kind of mug you'd expect to find in a boxing ring, where the Rod has in fact spent much of his time.

He takes a cursory glance around the assembled muscle dudes pumping up, and decides it's time. He lets his oversized flannel shirt fall to the floor, and the friendly banter, the clanking of weights, the squirt of baby oil onto taut muscled flesh all stop. The Rod keeps his face stony but on the inside he smiles. The mind fuck has begun.

There are whispers of "Shit, man" and "What the fuck!" and "Mother of Christ."

After that, there is silence. The room is drinking in the Rod, dressed only in a pair of cutoff jeans that barely contain his tree-trunk legs, monster ass and a cock that's started to swell.

His body's a network of dense muscle fibers and crisscrossing veins. The Rod is synonymous with vascularity. He adjusts the grapefruit-sized bulge in his cutoffs and starts doing arm curls, barely noticing the weight he's easily heaving. His body swells larger. So does his crotch. Several of the room's muscle jocks swallow nervously.

The Rod drinks in the nervous attention, but only for a second. These dweebs are too easy, and the Rod's a man who likes a challenge. His gaze darts casually over the assembled bodybuilders, landing on the man he's searching for: Trey Trojan, Mr. Perfect, three-time Muscle Pump Champion. He's the man to beat.

Or the pussy to fuck, Rod thinks. Everyone else gives Mr. Muscle Pump apprehensive glances. Rod brazenly eyes him up and down. It's good to see the dude in person at last, not just his image plastered on the cover of a whack of muscle rags, his pretty boy smile as shiny as his polished bod. In person he looks even better.

Mr. Perfect is a steel statue come to life. His waist is tiny, his shoulders ridiculously wide, his pecs firm yet bouncy, all in symmetry with his thick arms and thicker legs. Even his calves, a common weak spot, flare like upside-down teardrops. All this muscle is draped tightly in smooth skin bronzed to perfection, with one thick vein running over each bicep. Boyish blond hair cascades across his high cheekbones. He's just turned twenty and looks like the freshest of meat.

The other bodybuilders shudder. One look at his Olympian physique, and everyone knows Trey Trojan is going to saunter away with another Mr. Muscle Pump title. The Rod shivers, but not out of awe. Unlike the suddenly meek muscle boys in their banana thongs, he's after a trophy the judges can't award.

Trey struts his way, basking in every reflection he catches of himself from the mirrors lining the room.

"What are you looking at?" Mr. Muscle Pump snaps. So, the kid's talking to him. Who knew there was room within his self-obsessed vanity to notice anyone else? The Rod pretends to stare dumbly at the boy and doesn't respond. Someone with more brains and less self-assurance than Mr. Muscle Pump would have realized the larger man was just biding his time.

"Great, another retard," the champ snorts, earning nervous laughter from the other muscle boys.

The Rod smiles a wicked smile, and a hush falls on the room. Mr. Muscle Pump doesn't notice.

He steps in front of the Rod to admire himself in a mirror. He wears an eye patch–sized baby blue posing pouch. His navel pouts as it pokes out from the hard ridges of his abs. He strikes a Most Muscular pose. Striations fill his chest, his smile dazzles and his teeny trunks disappear into the crack of the most gorgeous ass the Rod has ever seen. It's thrust tauntingly toward him, flexing and filling with ridges of definition. Before the competition is done, the Rod knows, he's going to fuck that ass.

His strong hand settles on Mr. Muscle Pump's rounded delt. The blond straightens in surprise, looking up at the Rod.

"Nice panties," the Rod growls. "Where'd you get 'em? Victoria's Secret?"

The kid's face turns snotty.

"Do you know who I am?"

"I do," the Rod replies, a mean grin spreading over his rough-hewn features. "But do you know what you're about to become?"

For just a second, Mr. Muscle Pump loses a fraction of his attitude—after all, the Rod towers over him and carries pounds more muscle—but then Trey reminds himself who the champion is.

"You need to learn some respect, freak," Trey begins. He never finishes the thought.

With a speed that belies his bulk, the Rod grabs the kid's nipples and squeezes. Shocked, Mr. Muscle Pump takes a wild and clumsy swing, but the Rod squeezes harder and Mr. Muscle Pump's bulging arm falls limp at his sides. Then Trey Trojan begins to quiver.

It's ludicrous, really. He's a light-heavyweight, which is still plenty big. When fully dressed, his arms pop his sleeves. His ass splits open his jeans. His pecs are a sweeping vista of slab muscle merging into a deep canyon—he could be titty fucked, no problem. Yet like many muscle boys who are obsessed with the perfect pump, he can be ruled through his nipples. The Rod squeezes harder.

"I'll tell," he quavers, his voice no longer deep, now whiny, like a brat from a boy band crooning to teenage girls while wetting his pants over their jock boyfriends.

"Tell who?" Rod demands.

There are all sorts of people the kid could complain to. Security. The judges. His mom. Apparently she's a pit bull of a woman. But the Rod knows that Mr. Three-Time Muscle Pump Champion is not going to say a word—certainly not by the time the Rod's done with him.

He twists his grip, Trey gasps in pain, and the bigger man lowers his arms, pulling the boy's nips into elongated tips.

"Stop," Trey hisses, the word barely heard.

It's too late. Mr. Perfect, his massive polished muscles squeezed into a pair of skimpy baby blue trunks, sweat now streaking his perfect tanned bod, falls to his knees, his mouth mere inches from the Rod's bulging crotch, still sheathed within his cutoff jeans.

The other muscle boys elbow each other, gasping and twittering.

A camera crew from a muscle website, taping some pump-room action, captures the whole thing.

"Lower my jeans," the Rod orders.

"No," Trey says, but his tongue, nervously licking his shapely lips, betrays him. The Rod tugs more forcefully on the kid's nipples. Mr. Perfect's meaty pecs bob up and down. Trey could call for help or put up a fight. He's the champ and could have the Rod booted from the competition. Instead, Trey Trojan's muscled arms move like they're on marionette strings, fumbling with the Rod's belt and the buttons of his cutoffs, slowly pulling them open. The Rod's cock tumbles out. His cutoffs stay on.

The Rod's not wearing posing trunks. Doesn't need 'em. At no point did he intend to step on stage. This is where the real competition, and the real champion, will be chosen.

Mr. Muscle Pump gazes at the Rod's dangling sausage and huge balls. The blond bodybuilding star blushes, the flush flooding his face, running down his solid neck to the top of his massive pecs. But his pretty blue eyes do not look away. The Rod releases his hold on the kid's nipples; he gasps at the sudden rush of blood to his aching nips, and he looks ready to keel over. Instead, his face falls into the Rod's crotch. The kid immediately pulls away, shaking his blond hair as if to clear his senses, but it's too late—he's caught the Rod's scent, and there's no going back.

The Rod's cock thickens, and Trey's pupils dilate as the tip of the larger man's dick rises upward. Even semisoft, it's huge.

Mr. Muscle Pump stares. "It's too big," he murmurs, even though the Rod hasn't told him what to do with it. Yet.

The Rod slaps the kid's cheeks with his dick. Mr. Muscle Pump's eyes close in ecstasy as his lips absorb the spongy blows. The Rod's fully hard now, and Trey gazes in awe.

"I...I have to start pumping up," he stammers.

The Rod snorts and jerks his chin to the dumbbells on the floor.

"Who's stopping you?"

The two muscle men are surrounded by a wall of hard flesh. Guys with bigger dicks have pulled them out. Guys with steroid-shrunken balls keep theirs hidden but stroke themselves within their tiny trunks.

Trey, still on his knees, picks up the dumbbells, blushing now from head to toe, his skin glowing from within. The Rod knew the muscle boy would get off on being watched—he was built to perform in front of an audience. The weights clank and Mr. Muscle Pump's already rounded biceps pop even bigger, clenching into tight peaks at the top of each curl. And the more blood engorges his arms, the more his jaw loosens, hanging slack.

"Kiss it," the Rod commands.

Mr. Perfect presses his pouty lips to the tip of the Rod's cock, still pumping the weights, switching to overhead lifts, his massive shoulders clenching and unclenching.

"Lick it," the Rod orders.

The blond's tongue lolls out like a dog's, sliding up and down the Rod's shaft. The cock springs up ever harder, now so huge the kid pulls back. His throat undulates.

He begins doing triceps extensions, one dumbbell at a time.

"Suck it," the Rod demands.

"I told you...it's too big," Mr. Perfect gasps.

The other guys snort.

"Come on, pussy," a meathead with a crew cut scoffs. "You know you want it."

The other guys snigger. The Rod's not the only one who's had it with Mr. Muscle Pump's attitude.

Trey blushes and doesn't know where to look, so the Rod helps him. He takes the tip of Trey's chin, lowers it, takes aim, and shoves his cock deep down Mr. Muscle Pump's throat. It's like the kid's been hit by lightning. His entire body begins to shake, every muscle in his body clenching and unclenching. He drops the dumbbells. He doesn't need them now to get a pump. From his massive flexing pecs to the tensed glutes tumbling out of his baby blue trunks, down to his enormous quads and calves, his entire body flexes and unflexes as if he were being hit by electricity. It's the best pump of his life.

His throat opens like a valve and with a mind of its own it swallows the Rod's rod like a starving man given his first taste of food. He claws at Rod's tree-trunk legs, gripping them so that he can get a better angle, shoving his head up and down on the massive dick, the muscles he's worked on so hard continuing their spastic flexing dance.

Whatever else one may say about Mr. Perfect, he has stamina. The Rod's pretty sure he could go all day. And indeed he will, if the Rod gets his way, which he always does—on his terms.

He shoves the kid off him. Trey falls flat on his ass, shuddering a few more times from his all-body muscle flex before settling into ripped relaxation. He looks more amazing than ever. The other bodybuilders stop their mocking to stare. Trey's abs are taut peaks and valleys, rippling into his trunks. His nipples are chewable tips set atop pecs that are heaving with labored breathing and dripping in sweat.

Trey wipes the Rod's glossy precum from his mouth.

He looks at the muscle studs gazing down at him. He's Mr. Muscle Pump, here to defend his title, suddenly flat on his ass.

"I need to get oiled," he says, his voice deep and trembling only slightly. Already he's getting his attitude back. He tries to stand, but the Rod kicks his legs out from under him. "Please," he begs, "I have to go onstage soon."

There's a pathetic crack to the blond's voice that makes the larger man smile.

"You heard the chump," the Rod says to the assembled muscle men, "I mean *champ*. He needs oil."

A dozen dicks are out in a flash, though none of them come close to the Rod's. Muscular forearms start pumping away.

"What? No, I..."

Trey's words are useless. These guys are loaded with hormones, and their shots of cum explode, splashing over Mr. Perfect's pumped body in huge gobs, white cum trickling down his tanned muscle tits. The Rod grabs a bottle of baby oil, squirting the clear liquid over Mr. Perfect.

"Rub it in," the Rod orders, and the young muscle champ obeys, coating himself with cum and oil. Only then does the Rod notice a wet spot forming from within Trey's baby blue trunks. The dude's spooged himself!

"Number Twenty-two," an announcer calls, "Next contestant, Number Twenty-two, Mr. Trey Trojan."

Trey hesitates, still on his knees, gazing up at the Rod, afraid he'll pummel him if he tries to move. His eyes dart hungrily for the stage.

"Well," Rod barks, "get going."

Trey scrambles to his feet, and the Rod gives him a hard shove in the ass with one foot, leaving a clear footprint on the satiny trunks. Trey almost falls but catches himself, his bulging ass wiggling as he stumbles out onstage.

The Rod watches Mr. Muscle Pump's posing routine. As Christina Aguilera croons "Beautiful," the three-time champ moves smoothly from a side biceps to a gorgeous lat spread and into his patented tit squeeze, grimacing wildly until it looks like all those amazing muscles are about to explode. As the music stops, he holds his hands up to wave to the wildly cheering fans.

He emerges backstage high as a kite, riding the endorphins from flexing his muscles in the spotlight, the cries of the crowd driving him wild, the smell of cum filling him with a rush. Sweaty spooge soaks his posing trunks. He's so fucking hot the Rod practically rapes him on the spot.

Mr. Muscle Pump spots the Rod, and the blond blushes instantly, the memory of his subservience dimming his euphoria.

He tries to sidestep the larger stud, but the Rod catches one of the pumped boy's iron biceps in his viselike grip.

"I hear you just got a perfect score for that performance."

"I did?" The need in his voice is plaintive.

"Sure," the Rod lies, having no clue. "First time that's ever been done."

"It is?"

Glancing down, the Rod sees Mr. Muscle Pump has sprung a wee woody, the youngster's small dick pushing his microtrunks out by barely an inch. The Rod snorts in contempt—and lust. This is going to be an amazing fuck. Small-dicked guys are always the best.

"It's too bad," the Rod says. "Perfect score now means you peaked too early. Now you're screwed. No way you can blow 'em away in the pose down."

Mr. Muscle Pump's brow crinkles in confusion, not following the logic. *Only someone this pretty could get away with being so dumb*, thinks the Rod

"You've always got to save the best for last. The judges are going to score you tougher than ever."

Now Mr. Muscle Pump gets it, and his little hard-on shrivels.

"Is...is there anything you can do to...to help...you know..."

His words trail off, and for a second the Rod plays dumb, drawing out the champ's discomfort.

"Oh," he says, "you mean to get you more pumped? I don't know. I don't think you could handle it."

"Please," Mr. Muscle Pump begs, "I'll do anything you say."

"Please what?" the Rod says.

Mr. Muscle Pump looks like a tenth-grade holdback stuck in advanced physics. His polished pecs heave as he tries to divine what's expected of him. The Rod leans in close, his own over-hanging chest rubbing against Trey's, muscle on muscle. The Rod cups Mr. Muscle Pump's undersized crotch.

"You should stuff this with a sock, instead of that boy dick. I've seen six-year-olds with bigger cocks."

Mr. Muscle Pump hangs his head, not sure where to look.

"There are two kinds of bodybuilders in the world," the Rod continues, "The men, and the boy bitches. Want to guess which one you are, micro-dick?"

Trey blushes again from head to toe. He looks ready to pull away, but he wants to win.

"I'm a boy bitch," he says, biting his lip.

The Rod slides his free hand down Trey's spine, getting lots of oil on his thick fingers as they disappear into the smooth cleft of Mr. Muscle Pump's ass. The Rod saws up and down in that crack, against the muscle champ's warm hole. Mr. Muscle Pump groans and involuntarily gyrates his ass as he leans into the Rod, wrapping his arms around the older man's thick neck for balance and resting his head into the crook of his shoulder.

"I'm a boy bitch," he says loud enough for everyone to hear, and then adds, "Sir."

"Now drop your panties," the Rod orders.

Mr. Muscle Pump hesitates, eyes darting nervously around. The Rod screws his finger into the boy's pucker, making him grunt and stand on tiptoes.

"Yes, sir," he says meekly, squealing as the Rod shoves his finger in all the way. The boy is hard again.

Mr. Muscle Pump shimmies his trunks down. Once they're off his ass they flutter to the ground, and he steps out of them like a show dog.

"Turn around," the Rod orders.

Trey's head and shoulders droop, but his little dick stays

hard as a rock as he faces the crowd of bodybuilders. There are whoops, sniggers and faint applause. Mr. Muscle Pump is truly on display, stripped of the one thing that hid the only part of his body he couldn't make any bigger. His crotch is shaved clean, as silky smooth as the rest of him, and just as deeply tanned—he went into the fake-and-bake booth buck naked, and probably threw a woody each and every time.

The Rod undoes his shorts with his free hand and grips his massive cock. His fingers can't circle all the way around it. He grabs some oil off Trey's dripping man tits and rubs it over his dick. He lines up the massive head against Mr. Muscle Pump's pulsating hole, which practically pants in fear and anticipation, opening and closing of its own volition. The Rod shoves hard, piercing deeply into Mr. Muscle's Pump's velvety insides.

Trey gasps. "It's too big!" He thrashes wildly, desperate to get off the Rod.

The Rod grabs the blond's hair and yanks his head toward the mirror. Mr. Muscle Pump still pants and struggles, but his eyes are locked on the image before him. His body looks even better than before. He trembles around the Rod's huge dick, watching every one of his own muscle fibers flexing tight. At the same time he's hyperventilating.

"Please…" he begs.

Not "please get off," just "please." Like any top worth the name, the Rod knows exactly what Mr. Muscle Pump is begging for.

"Grab him," the Rod orders a pair of hefty heavyweights.

The bodybuilders, both covered in tattoos, obey immediately, each pinning one of Mr. Muscle's Pumps arms and shoulders against their own granite physiques, immobilizing Trey with immovable walls of muscle. And then the Rod starts to really fuck him.

Mr. Muscle Pump whimpers like a trapped animal, desperately trying to escape the Rod's rapacious dick. He begs for the Rod to stop, for someone to help. The rest of the bodybuilders are too busy sliding their hands up and down their own dicks.

And then something snaps inside the muscle champ. His plaintive voice turns to solid grunts. He's no longer struggling against the tattooed bodybuilders, whose own engorged dicks are oozing cum. The Rod motions the two behemoths to back off, and one of them starts going down on the other. The Rod smiles. Now, *this* is a pump room.

Trey's rock-solid ass starts matching the Rod pump for pump, and, giving himself over to the fuck, he flexes his arms into a bulging double biceps. His body is crisscrossed with delicate vascularity and sweat drips down his chest and abs. His little dick looks ridiculous against his oversized—but perfectly proportioned—muscles. Dropping his arms, he feels himself all over, getting off on his own rock-hard body, his hands touching everywhere—except his undersized weenie.

"Oh, yeah, daddy, fuck me, fuck me, fuck me!"

The Rod feels his climax building and he grabs Mr. Muscle Pump's nipples, squeezing hard, sending the champ's ass into convulsions as the Rod shoots long and hard. The blond still hasn't come, and when he reaches for his own stubby dick, so red and swollen it appears painful, the Rod grabs his wrist.

"You'll ruin it," he says, jerking his head toward the mirror. "Leave your oversized clit alone."

The insult makes the champ's insignificant cock that much harder.

"But I can't go out with this," he whines, gazing at his hard-on.

The Rod snorts, pulling out. He uses the champ's baby blue trunks to wipe the cum off his dick. Spooge drips from Trey's taut butt.

"Put 'em on," the Rod orders, handing over the bikini bottoms. Mr. Muscle Pump obeys.

"Number Twenty-two, calling Number Twenty-two..." comes from the loudspeaker.

"You're up, chump. Who knows, if you do win, I may even give you a round two."

"Yes, sir!" Mr. Muscle Pump replies, the worship clear in his voice and in his puppy dog eyes. The rest of the bodybuilders in their banana slings don't snigger now. They look jealous.

Trey Trojan easily wins his fourth Muscle Pump Championship. Like a good show horse he immediately canters backstage, his little hard-on pushing up against his cum-soaked posing trunks. His pecs jiggle as he hurries toward the Rod.

Later, after the awards are presented, the Rod eyes the Muscle Pump trophy, which is nearly as tall as his muscle champ. There's a flexing gold bodybuilder in the middle of the gaudy prize, with an obelisk at the trophy's peak.

The Rod's going to enjoy shoving it up Mr. Muscle Pump's ass.

MUSCLE WORSHIP: IF I SAID YOU HAVE A BEAUTIFUL BODY, WOULD YOU HOLD IT AGAINST ME?

Jack Fritscher

Part 1

The Roar of the Muscle
The Smell of the Crowd

A lucky man with a normal body can be embedded inside muscle culture. For any curious initiates wanting to suck up the inside scoop on muscle worship, welcome to a fast introduction for muscle freaks. This brief true story, like a fast tutorial by a wine connoisseur, is an insider's guide to a particular species of gay sex that is accessible to men who are willing to travel through a homomasculine synergy of lust, ritual and archetype that allows them to genuflect to the muscular beauty of athletes' bodies.

Gay sex always has an element of worship. In the way that rap is the *lingua franca* of black culture, the platonic ideal of the perfect male body is the *lingua franca* of gay male culture. Each man as he comes out to himself finds his desires more revealed, until, if he is lucky, he is kneeling in adoration of the Greek statue of the perfect male body in the way that Blanche DuBois says, "Suddenly there is God so quickly."

There's no quiz at the end of this quick intro to the true story of how a guy with an ordinary body becomes lovers with a championship bodybuilder. For masturbators with an urgency to swing into the sweaty gymnastics of muscle sex, skip to part two. For men with eager questions about what it's like to connect sexually with the ideals of hero worship experienced in high school, and who want to step up to the grown-men's fraternity of hot, raw, naked muscle worship, fasten your seat belts.

Muscle is one means to an end of gay-male fulfillment. Frankly, for a gay man to die without delving into the Platonic beauties of musclesex may be some kind of existential sin against the queer necessity of pushing self-identity into the most supreme orgasm possible. Born a male, a man is gorgeously fated to learn what men are, and, in the hallelujah chorus of all that, he is fated to combust in the desire that he himself is part of all that fireworks essence, even at the risk of dying at the feet of the masculinity he worships.

American sports tend to be objective and subjective. In objective sports, the basketball drops or does not drop through the hoop. The tight end either catches the football or he doesn't. The tennis pro makes his serve or he misses. Objective sports may have referees and umpires, but they are mostly yes-or-no athletics. Everyone basically sees the same results.

Subjective sports like gymnastics, skating, fencing and body-building determine winners or losers not by definitive touch-downs, but by judges' opinions. Of all sports, bodybuilding is the least understood because it is the most subjective. If gymnas-tics has a right way to move on the flying rings, bodybuilding has several right ways to execute the mandatory poses that display the bodybuilder's various muscle groups separately and together.

Who wins a physique contest is often as much a trick question as which is the best art form: literature, painting or music. The results depend on subjective values and enthusiasms. Most Americans like their sports cut and dried. For that reason, bodybuilding has been slow in coming to national acceptance as more than a cult sport. Someday it will, when Calvinism dies, and when it does, bodybuilding will finally become an Olympic event.

Physique presentation is a sporting objectification of self that is art and science, logic and feeling. A bodybuilder needs to know his body. He is dancer, actor, salesman. He is a contradiction in terms: a romantic existentialist. He strides barefooted across the stage with a dozen other bodybuilders. He takes his place in the lineup. He stands pumped and oiled and nearly naked, pouched confidently into his tiny posing briefs. He poses without movement, a perfectly sculpted statue. He radiates victory. He asserts his Command Presence under the hot lights. He calls the eyes of judges and audience to the quality edge of his muscle. Size. Symmetry. Power. Proportion. Bulk. Definition. Striation. Vascularity. Grooming. Look. His superior Command Attitude reduces the other highly competitive muscle to beefcake. As much as drag queens can sing the anthem, "I Am Who I Am," his posture states, "Here I am!"

Winners know how to peak for the contest day. Three weeks before competition they cut carbohydrates from their high-protein diet to remove the last micro-pinch of body fat that might obscure muscle display. Workouts intensify to carve out the lean definition of each separate muscle in the bulked muscle groups. A week before, the entire body is strip-shaved for the first time to allow any cuts or shaving rash to heal. In the last forty-eight hours, diuretics drain the minute layer of water between the muscle and the skin. The skin, paper thin, form fits the striae of each muscle, showing the minutest furrow like tiny grooves on granite. The vascularity of the veins snakes around the muscle almost on top of nearly invisible skin. The tan, by contest day, must be perfect and the body smoothed by a final shave before it is oiled backstage.

Contests are grueling twelve-hour affairs. The prejudging, where the contest is actually won or lost, begins at ten in the morning, and, depending on the classes, Teenage, Men, and Weight and Age Divisions, can last until the early afternoon. By the evening show at eight, the judges, of whom there must be at least five, have tallied their votes. The prejudging audience, smaller and hard core, can only have guessed at the winner. The audience for the evening show is larger, fans and friends and family, hot to party and cheer the parade of muscle bodies and wait eagerly for the names of the four finalists and the winner.

In the morning, the contestants arrive early. They saunter into the green room. They check in disguised under thick jogging suits and bulky nylon athletic jackets. They carry enormous gym bags. Some arrive alone. Some have the company of their training partners or their coaches.

The room is silent. Brows furrow with concentration. They psych each other out. One by one they begin the slow strip of their jackets and gym shoes and sweatshirts and T-shirts and sweatpants. Each reveals his stuff slowly. The offstage competition posing has begun.

Arms, big guns appear. Broad shoulders. Huge pecs. Washboard abs. Thunder thighs. Big, naked bubble butts. In unshaven groins, penises sprout tight with tension or hang long and thick with languorous confidence.

Attentive buddies fold the contestants' clothes into the gym bags. They wet their hands with baby oil and begin the even slather of the huge muscle bodies. The bodybuilders slide into their nylon posing briefs. Most pull their penises straight up toward their navels and let their balls hang low in the pouch. They pin the small white paper with their contest number over the front left hip of their briefs.

This is ritual.

Some play tug-of-war with their partners, pulling white towels back and forth to bring up the day's glossy pump on their years of hard muscle building. Others move to the ton of iron delivered to the theater for the day to polish their muscle, most often their arms, one last time before marching out onstage for the real competition of group comparison, flexing in unison mandatory poses, then individually, each one mounting the dais alone to pose for sixty seconds to music of his own selection.

Part 2
The Spray of Flashbulbs
225 Pounds in a 2-Ounce Speedo

Ryan, driving the Corvette from San Francisco to San Diego, could only guess what lay in store for him and his bodybuilder lover. That first morning of their first contest, when he and Kick entered the greenroom, Ryan thought he had died and gone to heaven. He was surrounded by more than twenty naked body-builders. He tried to keep custody of his eyes. He folded Kick's clothes and knelt at his feet, oiling up his legs to his shoulders. Ryan, during a scene of musclesex, had convinced Kick to replace baby oil with olive oil, because its sheen was more lustrous and its essence more classic.

"Whatever you say, coach."

Kick was up. He thought it was a good omen that his assigned contest number was *One*.

The morning prejudging ran nearly three hours. Ryan was beaming. Kick glowed. They met during a break backstage.

"You look great out there," Ryan said.

"I feel great out there," Kick said. He motioned for Ryan to move in closer. "Spread some more oil on my chest." He pointed toward the watch pocket in Ryan's Levi's. "Give me a hit," he said. He reached into Ryan's pocket for a small snifter of coke. He blew two lines. "Now you," he said.

"I'm already wired," Ryan said.

"Come on." Kick put his arm on Ryan's shoulder. The heady smell of contest sweat and olive oil made Ryan's tits ache. "We're here to have a good time."

Ryan swacked off the snifter.

"Again," Kick said.

Ryan snorted another line.

"It's good for the vascularity," Kick said. He thrust his arms, fists down, alongside his thighs, flexed, and popped his veins. "Nice, huh?"

"Sexy."

"I want you to know," Kick said, "how much fun it is to be inside this body." He chucked Ryan under the chin.

"Every man on that stage would like to be in your body. They might as well go home. You're going to win."

"I know."

After the prejudging, Ryan drove Kick in the Corvette to a coffee shop. Kick ordered an orange juice with four raw eggs. Ryan ordered but was too hyped to eat.

"Keep your strength up," Kick said. "You want to shoot a terrific video tonight." He stroked his high-top gym shoe up and down Ryan's leg. "Muscle TV."

Kick was triumphant in his evening posing routine. Through his video monitor, Ryan caught every graceful nuance. He knew

the choreography he had coached by heart. He had even selected
Kick's music. He was bored with uninspired muscleheads posing
one after the other to the clichéd themes from *Exodus, Rocky,
Star Wars* and *Superman*. Ryan chose Tchaikovsky's "Marche
Slav." Its thunderous power matched Kick's smooth and
commanding posing routine.

He flexed. He shined. He was pure, hard, blond muscle.
His hair and face and jaw accentuated the blond brush of his
mustache, groomed trooper sharp. His physique flowed from
his head. He hit each pose hard. He had appeal. There was no
quiver from the muscle exertion or the coke. He displayed every
body part alternating always with the dozen ways he powered
out his arms.

The crowd called out for more.

He hit the Most Muscular pose three times and threw his
arms up over his head in victorious salute. The muscle crowd
rose cheering to their feet.

Here was a man.

"All right, gentlemen," the head judge said over the loudspeaker. "We're calling the five finalists out on stage for a pose
down. This is the final comparison, man for man, to determine
the winner. Ladies and gentlemen, these are our five finalists.
Number One, Kick Sorensen..."

Ryan heard no other names.

The five finalists strolled out onstage. Each picked a spot
and hit a pose, playing the cheering audience. Kick owned stage
center. He threw a double-biceps shot and then crunched down
into the popular Most Muscular. The crowd went wild.

"Give yourselves some room, fellas. Spread out. Make sure
you're in the light."

The finalists sought their places. Kick held center stage with
two musclemen moving to each side. They all stood heels close

together, toes pointed out, elbows extended, arms hanging
down.

"All right. Let's do a double-biceps pose on three. I want you
all to hit exactly the same pose at the same time. On three. One-
two-three. Hit your pose."

Kick raised both arms. His biceps peaked under the hot light.
He was arms and more than arms. He worked his pecs. He tightened his abs. Always he was working his legs. Contests are won
or lost on legs.

"Okay. A lat spread from the front. On three. One-two-
three."

Kick positioned his thumbs behind his waist with his fingers
front pointing down his hips. He swung his elbows out, lifted his
chest, spread his shoulders and opened wide his lats, holding the
pose, then twisting slightly from the waist, left to right, catching
the best play of the light.

"Now a side-chest pose. Your favorite side. Take your positions. Quiet, please. We want a side-chest shot. Rotate the sides.
One-two-three."

Kick stood on his left foot and the ball of his right with his
right knee bent to display his right calf development. He turned
his head to face the judges straight on. He clasped his hands
above his right hip and pulled his left shoulder toward the audience. His arms read like an awesome frame around his massive
pecs.

"Now a side-tricep. Your favorite side. Take your positions.
On three. One-two-three. Hit it."

Again, standing sideways, yet facing the judges, Kick rested
on his left foot. He placed the ball of his right foot behind him,
flexing his calf. He shot his right arm down his outside thigh,
displaying the horseshoe definition of his triceps. Then reaching
his left hand behind his butt, he shifted the pose, taking hold

of the hand facing the crowd to pop his tricep even more. He instinctively knew the extra flourish needed to show off the fine detail of each muscle to its best advantage.

"And relax. Turn toward the curtain, please. Give yourselves room, fellas. Spread out. Okay. Double-bicep from the rear. On three. One-two-three. Hit it."

Kick was born to show arms. From the backside, his biceps mounded like twin baseballs on the girth of his huge arms. He powered into the biceps shot, spread his shoulders and kicked in a rearview of his left calf.

"Gentlemen, let's have a back lat spread. On three. One-two-three. Hit it."

Kick thrust his butt out. His perfect glutes caught the light. A woman behind Ryan screamed. Kick tucked his thumbs behind his waist and opened his elbows, wide, spread his back, slightly at first, and then opening the left side to its full plane, and then the right, both wings from his waist to his shoulders in perfect symmetry. The back of his blond head glowed atop the column of his thick neck.

"Relax. Face front, please."

The crowd had settled on a favorite. Someone set up a chant of "Number One! Number One!" The number Ryan had pinned on Kick's brown nylon briefs.

"May we have some quiet, please? Face front, please. May I remind you, Number Three, that these are mandatory poses. If you're not sure which way to turn, look at the men next to you."

The crowd cheered and hooted.

"All right now, fellas. Flexing the legs, display the thighs. One-two-three."

Kick locked his hands behind his head, elbows wide, armpits rampant. He flashed his washboard abs and thrust one leg and then the other out for judgment. The thickness of his thighs broke up into distinctly displayed muscle groups. The contestant on his right moved his own leg toward Kick's, daring closer comparison. The crowd went wild. Kick lowered his hands to his waist, thrust his leg toward his competitor, flexed it, looked at the other bodybuilder, then pointed, grinning, to his own thigh, bulked, carved, cut, vascular and tanned. He looked up from his leg and threw the crowd a devastating so-what-do-you-think grin.

"And relax. Fellas, we're going for your favorite ab shot on three. One-two-three. Hit it."

Again Kick locked his hands behind his head. The crowd was with him. He kicked out his right leg, resting his foot on the heel, working his leg length, giving more than required, locking his abs into the sculpted ridges Ryan's tongue knew by heart. He carved his abs tight, then sharpened them tighter. The crowd chanted "Number One!" Kick's whole posture, arms up, leg extended, belly displayed, seemed to focus the light on the full pouch of his posing briefs. Ryan, at the last minute in the greenroom, had slipped Kick's balls and cock through a brass cock ring to accentuate the big package. "I want them to see everything you've got," he had said. He wondered how much a big cock and balls registered with the judges, many of whom were older, closeted gay men. Onstage, Kick radiated pure sex. Women in the crowd were shouting, "We want Number One!"

Ryan shouted into the din. "Dream on!"

"And relax. Catch your breath, fellas. We're going to do the Most Muscular now. Your favorite Most Muscular. On three. One-two-three. Hit it."

Kick raised his arms wide, elbows above his shoulders, then slowly, hunched, leaned over, and powered down into the Most Muscular crab pose. His right leg led his left. His arms were

Most Muscular. His chest pumped like a barrel. His head was up. His face back. His chin out. The cords in his neck spoke power. The crowd loved him. He broke the pose and hit it again. Then again. This last time in full lockdown, revolving his fists one around the other to play the brute force of his upper body and massive arms.

"And relax. Now there will be sixty seconds of free posing. Remember, fellas, this is a pose down. This is your final chance to show why you should be Mr. Western Pacific Coast. Take your sixty seconds. Use it, please."

The disco music came up over the cheers of the crowd. Each contestant tried to outpose the other. They moved, freestyle, pose against pose, topping each other: arms, chests, backs, abs and legs. They moved sideways. They turned front and back. Kick stayed confidently in place in the melee. He had found the best light. He was center to the group. They were good. But he was power. They were competitors, but he was brooking no competition. He ignored them jockeying into him, following his poses, trying to lure him into following their competitive moves. Instead, he grinned, thrust out his chin. His blond hair and his mustache glowed. He played straight to the audience, straight to the judges, straight to Ryan behind his video camera in the first row. Kick was surrounded by bodybuilders, but he was more than a bodybuilder. He was a Lord of Light.

The crowd turned to near riot. Fans with cameras rushed the lip of the stage. Applause. Whistles. "Number One!"

The minute of blasting music stopped. The crowd rose cheering louder. The head judge called for quiet. The auditorium soothed down expectantly. Finally, he named the fifth and fourth and third runners-up. The three men took their trophies, kissed the girl who presented them, and moved off to the side. Kick flexed his pecs and ran his hand down his rippled belly. The hall grew tense. Expectant. Kick stood next to Number Nine. He reached out to shake Nine's hand. Calls for "Number One!" flared here and there from the orchestra and balcony. "Number One!" Time stood still.

Ryan knew there was no God if they came this close and lost. In the pause, Number Nine hit his best Most Muscular. Kick raised both fists into his best double-biceps shot of the night and killed the guy with his arms.

"Number One! Number One! Number One!"

"Quiet, please." The judge was a sadist. "We have three trophies to award before we announce the winner of the Mr. Western Pacific Coast Contest." Ryan knew. He knew that he knew the verdict. "The trophy for Best Legs goes to Number One, Kick Sorensen!"

Kick hit a severe leg pose then threw his arms up in salute. Number Nine reached to shake his hand. The young blonde woman carried the Best Legs trophy to Kick. She leaned forward to give the winner his customary kiss. Ryan watched Kick deftly turn his mouth away. The blonde air-bussed his cheek. Kick set the trophy down at his feet.

"The trophy for Best Arms," the trophy Kick coveted most, "Number One, Kick Sorensen."

Kick hit a single side-biceps pose. The crowd cheered. He was sweeping the competition. Number Nine realized he was going to place second. Kick received the second trophy from the blonde girl and placed it near the first.

"Number One! Number One!"

Kick was a generous poser. He obliged the cheers, roiling a double-bicep shot down into one last Most Muscular pose. Number Nine, a sport to the end, followed suit. The audience screamed as Kick took the trophy for Best Posing.

Under the roar, the judge's words were lost as he named the

second runner-up. Number Nine heard. He raised his arms in valedictory and turned to shake Kick's hand.

The audience rose screaming to their feet.

"The winner of the Mr. Western Pacific Coast title is... Number One! Kick Sorensen!"

Ryan nearly died. "Omigod! I love you, Kick!"

Kick pumped off a succession of killer poses. He raised his prizewinning arms high over his head. The cheering rose as he accepted his First Place trophy and headed toward the posing platform. He mounted the dais and placed the four trophies at his feet. The four finalists grouped themselves on the platform's lower levels with Kick in top place. Photographers crowded to the foot of the stage to shoot the winners with cameras and flash guns.

Ryan toyed with his own anonymity. "Wasn't that Number One somethin'?" he said to a small group of three huge power-lifters.

"Yeah," they said.

"I hear this is his first contest." Ryan cast bread on the water.

"You're shittin' me." The guy curled his twenty-inch bicep up to stroke his thick mustache.

"Not me," Ryan said.

"Then the guy's even more of a dude." He turned to his partner. "Hey, Doyle. This is blondie's first contest." Then he saluted Ryan with his big meat hook. "Yeah, buddy."

That night Ryan drove the red Corvette, crammed with the four big trophies, back to the Motel San Diego. Laughing and exhausted, Ryan stripped and lay back on the bed.

"Lie still, coach." Kick arranged the muscle trophies carefully on the sheets around him.

"Now I know," Ryan was hot with anticipation, "what Oscar winners do when they get home."

Kick, smiling, moved back from the bed. Slowly, sensually, he stripped himself out of his green Adidas warm-up suit. His tanned body still glistened with the olive oil and sweat of the competition. With his thumbs, he pulled his tailored brown posing briefs down from his waist, down past the brass cock ring circling the root of his big blond dick and balls, down his official Best Legs in Ten Western States.

He had become very serious. For a moment, he stood and studied Ryan who was awestruck at this intimacy following so quickly the public physique presentation. The applause was nothing compared to what they saw in each other's eyes. In all their private nights of making love, no night had begun with such wide-open celebration of Kick's exquisite manliness. The world for the first time had acknowledged what they had privately known and pursued so intensely for so long together. The victory belonged to them both. They were united. They had gone public in their quest for manly excellence, and the crowds were eating it up.

Naked, in his All-American prizewinning glory, Kick moved toward the bed. He lowered himself slowly down on Ryan's naked body.

"I've wanted all my life to do this," Kick said. "This way. This time. On a night like this. Tonight's a special one."

He meant make muscle-love man-to-man, lover-to-lover, bodybuilder-to-coach, in those triumphant first hours after the winning of his first physique contest. Their separate boyhood dreams of manhood had conjoined.

"It's you, Ry. This is my personal best. From me to you. There's no other man."

At the start, the only promise they had made was never to become ordinary to each other.

"I want to lay it all on you, coach."

The energy between them was stronger than ever.

Hours later, exhausted in each other's arms, in the quiet before the San Diego dawn, Kick whispered to Ryan.

"You won't laugh," he said. He rubbed Ryan's belly frosted with dried glaze. "I mean it seriously."

He moved his golden face in close to Ryan's and announced it like a mandate to the writer whose cheek rested in the fragrant under-cove where Kick's arm and shoulder joined his chest.

"Someday," Kick said, "I want us to be a story told at night in beds around the world."

Ryan's hungry heart came running.

Part 3
Sport-Fucking
Romancing the Stoned

In gay sex, more is more.

In gay muscle-worship sex, more is the perverse divine.

Three months later, and very late on a spring night, after watching Arnold Schwarzenegger as Conan nailed up naked to the Tree of Woe, Kick was inspired to play an exotic sex scene. At first they joked about it, but the laughing fell away and the night grew serious. It was typical of the way they had sex. Kick poured them each a hit of the ecstatic drug their dealer nick-named Kryptonite.

"I only want half a hit," Ryan said.

"Name your poison," Kick said.

They toasted one another with the wineglasses. "To Arnold," Kick said. "And to us."

They had both liked the scene in which the muscle-warrior Conan, captured by the evil priest James Earl Jones, was cruci-fied to the mammoth stump of a huge tree on a barren primeval plain. Ryan grew excited as the image of Kick crucified grew between them. They began their preparations. Kick slowly stripped. Ryan anointed his body with olive oil to a high glaze.

In the basement room of the Victorian where they played before three full-length mirrors under the track-light spots, huge horizontal beams crossed over the heavy upright wooden foundation posts. They stood, both naked, before the crossed beams in the center of the room. Ryan fashioned a small linen loincloth that he wrapped around Kick's muscular waist, then dropped down to create a pouch for his dick and balls. He pulled the long, twisted length of linen up the crack of his ass and knotted the cloth to the waistband in the small of his back.

"I want to look stronger than Conan," Kick said. "I want us to get more intense than the movie. Let's see what a real muscle-beast restrained by steel looks like."

Ryan cinched Kick's wrists into heavy leather cuffs. Ryan's dick grew hard at the prospect of a new worshipful view of the man who relied on him to create the most private of the fantasies he could not perform alone.

Kick smiled at him. "Now you know why I love you," he said. "Now you know why, when I heard about you and read your stories, I had to meet you."

Ryan, the acolyte, led Kick to the beams. He placed a short wooden barrel at the foot of the cross. He gave Kick a hit of popper.

"I love you," Kick said, "for this, and more than this." He looked deep into Ryan's eyes. "You know, don't you! You *know!* You understand the Gift. It's not always in a man's body the way it is in mine. But more than my body, it's in my head. You're one of the few men who know I have a head."

"I love you," Ryan said.

The Kryptonite ecstasy was coming on. Ryan raised Kick's

huge arm and dug his tongue into the sweat steaming in his armpit. His mind swirled with images of ideal men, men without whom the world would be an intolerable place.

Kick mounted the barrel. His calves, sculpted to the perfection of inverted hearts, bulged as he rose up to position himself. He turned, as he always turned on the posing platform, arms held loosely akimbo from his massive shoulders, his hands hanging down, thumbs in, eight inches out from his thighs, and looked down at Ryan. He flexed his pecs: the muscles striated and defined and rolled, up, then down his chest. His dick tented the soft linen loincloth. His smile at Ryan was triumphant. There was no shame in this crucifixion.

Ryan administered them both a hit of popper. Kick's face, in the low track light, began to morph into the face of the idealized young Christ, stripped and crucified, whom Ryan had worshiped since boyhood. He had been trained at Misericordia to be an *alter Christus,* another Christ, but he knew he'd never be another Christ.

He realized a special revelation.

It was not himself; it had never been himself; it was Kick who was the *alter Christus.*

"I'm stoned. I'm stoned. I'm stoned," Ryan repeated to himself. "This is so crazy...." But the vision would not vanish.

"Tight," Kick said. "Tie me tight. I want to feel this." He nodded toward the three body-length mirrors. "I want to see this. I want to show you a show I've never shown anyone before."

Ryan tied Kick's ankles together and then wrapped the rope around the rough-hewn post.

"I want to take it as long as I can," Kick said. "I want to feel the full glory of muscular restraint."

Ryan tied Kick's huge arms wide open on the cross. Kick raised his head and breathed. His chest expanded. Sweat rolled down his face and dripped on his pecs. His cock writhed in the small linen loincloth.

Ryan offered him, the way Christ on the cross had been offered vinegar mixed with opium on a sponge, a double hit of coke. Kick snorted, then relaxed. He twisted one hand to a more comfortable angle on the cross.

"I'm ready," Kick said. "I want you to see a musclebeast more glorious than you've ever imagined."

Ryan pulled the barrel out from under his lover's feet. Kick's muscles tensed. His whole body, hanging under the strain, and triggered by the rush of the coke, took on a pump and vascularity so supernal that Ryan fell to his knees at the foot of the cross. He watched his lover strain and flex like a muscular Olympic gymnast performing the crucifix on the double rings. *I always thought,* Ryan's head swirled, *that it was me who was to be crucified.*

He serviced them both with popper.

Kick locked into a massive body flex. His loincloth, heavy with sweat, fell away under the strain of his muscle. His dirty-blond cock jutted straight forward over his massive thighs. He took a huge breath and let go. He hung, by his massive arms, crucified, head back and haloed by the shine of the track light. Ryan knelt before the sweating muscleman, cruciform above him. He took himself in his right hand and began to stroke his own hardening flesh. The moment grew mystical as Kick struggled, flexed, relaxed, flexed and endured against the hard wooden cross.

It started as night games: heroic sculpture from drawings and movies. It became some ritual else. Their separate fantasies meshed in the flesh, then separated in their minds, coming back together, each traveling separately, traveling together, finding the Ecstasy, the Energy, the Entity, the boundaries, the limits.

Kick was a bodybuilder, crucified, displayed in all his muscular glory, straining against the bondage, flying with the bondage. Ryan was his coach, his lover, his priest. He worshiped Kick's body from the foot of the cross. Coke sweat poured down Kick's naked flanks. The hard rod of his manhood arched over Ryan. The blond man glowed in the spotlight. He began to moan under the weight of his own big body. He saw his own face in the mirrors, handsome over his hanging muscle body. He moaned the moan Ryan always knew meant he was entering the Energy. Ryan followed with his own cock. He clamped the clips on his own tits. He hit them both with popper and tongued his way down Kick's body to his feet.

This was no Imitation of Christ.

This was real.

Kick was more than an *alter Christus*.

He was the incarnation of the real Christ Himself.

Ryan rose from his knees. He licked the sacred sweat from the blond fur of the thighs. He touched his Savior's massive meat. He massaged it, stroked it, while he stroked himself, until Kick's huge prick, throbbing with the tension of the muscle bondage, glistened. His whole body tightened down into a cruciform Most-Muscular position. Ryan's greased hand stroked Kick up to the edge of cumming. Ryan readied himself, stroking faster, his face looking up lovingly at his crucified Savior. He could feel the power rising in the crucified's body. Then suddenly, the white clotted rain shot like saving grace from Kick's lordly rod. Ryan's mouth opened hungrily. In his own hand, his own flesh throbbed to a simultaneous climax.

"Oh, my God," he said. "Oh, my beautiful God."

Two days later, over coffee at the Castro Café, Ryan's longtime confidante, the drag theologian, Sister Ironica Herself, was less than perpetually indulgent: "What you gay boys won't do to have fun."

Part 4
"Je ne regrette rien."
Sooner or Later Every Bodybuilder
Hustles Muscle

They were too hot not to cool down. A year passed. The idyll ended. They had a gentlemen's parting that left a bit of the best of them in each of them. During the months that followed, Ryan had to smile when he read a personals ad in the back of the *Bay Area Reporter* listed under *Models for Hire*. He recognized Kick's way with words, and he recognized the thumbnail photo showing the model "Armstrong" from the neck down.

I AM ARMSTRONG! BIG GUNS. Feel them: thick, big ARMS, muscle-bulked heavily from sweaty workouts, their huge girth sported in a cotton T-shirt, or subtly concealed by shirt sleeves of well-washed flannel stretched across their mass, now stripped to reveal mounds of baseball biceps cabled with vascularity, and thick horseshoe triceps, growing bigger before your eyes, the pump of each successive flex further expressing the disciplined power of the life force that built them. With those Big Guns lifted high in full frontal display of arm muscle, feel them again. Feel the density of each striation as it's gathered down into the depths of muscle armpits rich with the heavy male scent of bodybuilder muscle sweat. After a bit of 420 smoke and popper, if you find your nose exploring the heights of those pits, if you can take that big muscular arm in one hand, and your dick in the other, and discover that between the stroking of the two that you're cumming, then we're both gonna have fun! I'm on my way to the gym now. If Big-Guns rap-n-jack-off makes you break into a sweat you can't cool off by yourself, contact me. Armstrong@ intro2muscleworship.cum

All models have a going rate, and no models are in more demand than musclemen. Kick was charging $200 a session, no time limit, safe sex only. Ryan, amused, figured that during the two years he and Kick were together, he had enjoyed, at five sessions a week, over $100,000 worth of free sex, and a million bucks of personal intimacy on the sport-fucking circuit. Every curve and taste and smell and vision of Kick's body existed inside his head like a 3D hologram he could enjoy forever.

THUNDER AND LIGHTNING

Cage Thunder

I was stretching and warming up in the ring, psyching myself for my match. The guy I was scheduled to wrestle was new to BG East and I hadn't met him in person. I had seen pictures of him, though, and he was gorgeous: young, twenty-three at most, with ripped abs, muscular legs and a stunning upper body. As soon as the Boss emailed me the pics, my dick had gotten hard. I emailed back, *Hell yeah I wanna wrestle him!*

And so here I was, back in the ring in Fort Lauderdale, waiting.

I glanced at the wall clock: quarter after eight. The kid was late.

I went back into my mind-space, focusing on my stretching. It felt good to stretch. I was always in such a rush to get through my workouts—when I managed to squeeze in time at the gym— that I never managed to really get a regular stretching routine going. I blocked everything out as I reached for my toes, bending at the waist and trying to lower my forehead to my knees. I heard a phone ringing but blocked the sound out. I glanced up as my torso lowered and caught a glimpse of myself in the mirror outside the ring. I gave myself a wink. *The twink is going down.*

"The kid canceled," the Boss said from outside the ring ropes. "Car trouble, he says."

"Car trouble my ass—chickened out is more like it," I replied, as my forehead finally came to rest on my knees. I could feel the stretch in my hamstrings, and I exhaled.

"You up for a rematch?" the Boss asked me as he tucked his cell phone back into his pocket.

I gestured at my ring attire. "All geared up with no one to beat on, Boss." I replied with a shrug, but my curiosity was piqued. BG East rarely, if ever, filmed rematches. "Who we talking about?"

His eyes glinted, and he raised an eyebrow. "Max Coleman."

My eyes narrowed.

I fucking *hate* Max Coleman.

Our original match was taped when we were both new to the company. It was a motel match, and to be honest, he completely kicked my ass.

But it wasn't really a fair fight. While we are about equal in wrestling skill, in a motel room a bigger guy has a definite advantage. To beat someone bigger in a small space, you either have to be more skilled or quicker than the big guy. I was giving up three inches in height and twenty pounds of muscle, and without a lot of room to maneuver, well, I didn't have a chance. The match didn't start out fair, either. He knocked on the door while the cameras were already rolling and I answered. We were supposed to trash talk each other, move over to where the mattresses made a makeshift arena, strip out of our shirts and shorts and get wrestling.

Instead, the moment the door opened he attacked. I wasn't expecting it; in seconds he had my shirt pulled up over my head, blinding me and tangling my arms, and then he started working me over. I was never in the fight, and when I was finally beaten down and couldn't continue I had to put up with the humiliation of him sitting on my chest while he flexed his massive arms and laughed at me.

"Did you really think you had a chance?" he had mocked me as he struck a double-bicep pose. "Look at these fucking guns!"

And as if that weren't enough, he gave my face a not-so-playful slap before he got off me and the camera was turned off.

This match was also before I started wearing masks, drawing from their power.

Ever since, I've wanted nothing more than to totally kick the shit out of him. I'd tried to arrange a private match in the ring, just the two of us—no cameras, no referee—him and me, two hours. Two climb in, one climbs out. He was always evasive. "What do I have to prove?" he'd taunt me in emails or on the BG East message board. "I already kicked your ass once. What would be different this time? Not a fucking thing."

And I would burn in anger.

So I gave the Boss a nasty smile and drove my right fist into my gloved left hand. "Yeah, I could handle another shot at Coleman. Will he have the balls to show up?"

I was wearing black leather gloves with the fingers cut out, a black leather mask with a white facial outline, black boots and kneepads and a flattering black pair of trunks with two silver lightning bolts on the front that met over my crotch and formed an arrow pointing down. I walked to the side of the ring that faced the mirror, and struck an all-muscle pose. I had a deep tan and was in great shape. I'd trained really hard and even managed

to watch what I ate in the weeks leading to the trip to Lauderdale. I'd trimmed my thick torso hair and I looked great.

"Oh, he's on his way." The Boss gave me his wickedest grin.
He picked up a digital camera. "Guess we might as well start
taking your portraits until he gets here."

We'd just wrapped up my portraits when there was a knock
on the gym door, and Jon, who was going to run the video
camera during the match, opened it.

I walked over to the ring ropes closest to the door and stared
at the hated Coleman as he swaggered into the gym.

He was two inches taller than me, at six foot one, wearing
a pair of sweatpants cut off at the knees and a T-shirt he'd
cut the sleeves from and ripped so it was open almost to the
waist. He didn't look at me as he walked in and shook hands
with Jon. The Boss left me standing, watching, and went to
talk to him. Coleman put his gym bag down and pulled the
shirt over his head. He was bigger than he had been when we'd
wrestled three years earlier. His big shaved pecs, thick shoulders and huge biceps were defined, veins popping out as he slid
his shorts down. He was wearing a pair of electric blue trunks
with a silver lightning bolt across the front. I smirked. *Lightning trunks to wrestle Cage Thunder, huh?* He pulled on socks
and began lacing up white boots. When he was finished lacing
them, he headed for the ring.

He was good looking, with dark blond hair trimmed close to
his scalp in an almost military style cut. His torso and legs were
completely hairless, and there was a big bulge in the front of his
trunks that I didn't remember from our original match. His skin
was tanned a dark golden brown, and as he climbed through the
ropes he looked over at me and gave me a big smile. "Hey, man,"
he said, dimples deepening in his cheeks. One of his bright blue
eyes closed in a wink. "Let's put on a good show, huh?"

I nodded and watched as he started posing for the Boss's camera. My cock stirred inside my trunks. This fucker's body was gorgeous. His biceps peaked as he them, veins bulging in his forearms and shoulders. I remembered how it felt to be trapped in his viselike bear hug, powerful arms putting pressure on my lower back until I thought it would snap, him tossing me around like I weighed nothing.

"All right, let's get some of the two of you together," the Boss commanded, and I walked over to the corner where he stood, with one boot up on the lower rope. "Stand chest to chest," he said, so I stepped in close to Coleman. Our chests were maybe an inch away from each other. "Perfect."

"I'm going to kick your ass again," Coleman whispered, smile never fading.

I didn't reply. He was trying to get inside my head, make me doubt myself. Not a chance. I looked at his meaty pecs, anticipating how great it would feel to put a claw hold on them. Everything about him was massive and muscled—and all that really meant to me was a bigger and better target.

We did a couple more shots of the two of us, and then the Boss told Jon to put the camera down. "All right, when we start taping, we're going to start with the camera on you, Max," he said. "Stand over in front of the mirror and flex—you know what to do."

"Yup," he replied.

"Cage, you're going to be in the locker room," the Boss went on. "When Max is through flexing, he'll call you out. You appear, give him the onceover, and then climb in the ring and head over to your corner. We'll ring the bell, and you start."

I nodded, climbing out of the ring and through the locker room door, pulling it shut. My heart was pounding. I'd been waiting three years for another shot at the musclehead. My traitorous cock was semihard, which pissed me off. Sure, he was hot. Sure, he had a great body, one of the best I'd ever seen up close and personal. But he was an asshole, and he was the enemy.

I wasn't going to lose to that son of a bitch again.

The locker room was hot and sweat started to bead under my mask. I tried to focus on what I had to do to win the match, breathing deep, clearing my mind. *Forget everything, just focus on kicking his ass.*

"Hey, Thunder, what are you doing in there? You afraid to come out and fight me, pussy?"

I shoved the locker room door open, slamming it against the wall as I stalked through the doorway, then stopped. I looked into the ring, challenging Max's arrogant, mocking, cocky grin. I pointed at him and then down at the mat. "You're going down, musclehead," I growled, and climbed through the ropes, heading over to my corner as he retreated to the corner opposite mine.

He flexed his arms. "You sure you want some of this?" He kissed each bicep in turn. "These big guns are gonna shoot you down and break you, little man."

Stay calm, he wants you to lose your temper so you'll lose focus.

The bell rang.

We circled each other. I stalked him slowly, while he danced on the balls of his feet, mouthing a steady barrage of taunts. "I'm gonna break you," he taunted me, the grin I'd learned to hate on his face. "I'm gonna tear you limb from limb."

We locked up in the center of the ring, collar and elbow, pushing each other back and forth until with a powerful thrust he backed me into my own corner. He was so damned strong! He shoved my upper torso up and backward until I was on my toes. He stood between my legs, his powerful arms forcing my straining arms up, exposing my entire torso—

And he slapped my face.

It wasn't a hard slap, just a pop, didn't hurt at all, but it was loud, and meant to be insulting. He laughed and danced backward to the center of the ring, gesturing for me to come forward. I did, my arms outstretched, and he darted through them, scooped me up, and body slammed me to the center of the ring.

All the air left my lungs and a bolt of pain shot through my body from my lower back. As I started to get to my feet, he scooped me up and dropped me again. My ears ringing, the pain in my lower back throbbing, he grabbed me by the chin and dragged me back up to my feet. Back into the air I went, and this time he dropped my lower back over his knee. My body bent in two as I rolled off, landing on my stomach.

Fuck, that hurts, damn it to fuck...

And as I tried to clear my head, he grabbed my left leg, tucked my foot under his armpit, and sat on my upper back, dragging my leg up into a single leg crab. I tried to push up, to take some of the weight on my free knee and release the pressure on my lower back as he started twisting my foot around.

I don't know...how...much....more...I...can...take....

I was just about to submit when he released my leg.

Gasping, shaking my head, I started crawling to my corner.

He kicked me in the back.

I dropped to the mat and rolled desperately for the corner.

I started pulling myself up by the ropes when his knee slammed into my back again.

The momentum drove me headfirst into the turnbuckle.

Dazed, I climbed up on the ropes. I was on my feet when he grabbed my arm and my chin and hoisted me up in a rack across his shoulders.

"What do you say?" he taunted me as he walked to the center

of the ring with me draped limp across his shoulders. My legs hung from one side, my head and arms from the other side, and my back...

He started doing squats. Every time he got down as far as he could, my back screamed in pain.

I struggled, tried to focus, tried not to let the pain get to me...

"I submit! I submit! I submit!"

He shrugged me off his shoulders and I dropped to the mat, sprawled, dazed and in extreme pain. I was vaguely aware of him posing over me, flexing his massive muscles, and then he kicked me in the side, rolling me over onto my aching back.

"Look at that!" he sneered, reaching down and touching my hard cock. "You're hard! You *like* getting your ass kicked by a big muscle stud, don't you?"

He hooked his fingers into my trunks, and with a hard yank, tore them off me.

I lay exposed.

He laughed and tossed my trunks outside of the ring.

"Any time you're ready for more, pussy." He reached down and smacked my face. Again, it was just a slap, hurting nothing more than my pride. But my face smarted. With a laugh, he walked over to his corner.

I rolled over to my corner, pulling myself up by the ropes yet again, taking deep breaths, stretching my aching back as I stared across the ring at him. He was smirking, contempt written all over his handsome face.

Turn the pain to rage.

I stared at him, aware that my cock was still hard, willing the pain away, my hatred for him spilling over.

He held his hands out and signaled me to come and get him.

With each step across the ring, my anger rose until I reached the other side, standing in front of him, my cock bouncing.

I drove my fist into his ripped abs.

"Is that all?" He laughed. "Come on, give it to me again! Give me your best shot!"

I slammed my fist into him again.

"I think I may have felt that," he mocked me and shook his head. "Steel, baby, they're steel. Give it another try."

I pulled my fist back, smiled to myself, and punched him as hard as I could.

Only this time, I connected with his balls.

His face turned red, his eyes bugged out, and I stepped aside as he collapsed to the mat. He rolled, clutching his nuts, moaning.

I walked over, hooked my fingers into his trunks, and yanked them off.

His hard, muscular ass was—well, spectacular.

I sat on his back, slipped his trunks around his neck, and yanked back.

He gasped, legs kicking as I pulled, leaning back to get my weight into it.

"How them muscles working for you now, stud?" I taunted him as he tried to get air into his lungs. "Ain't such a big man now, are you?"

"You...cheating...*fuck!*" he somehow gasped.

I let go of his trunks and slammed his head onto the mat, then tossed the trunks outside the ring and rolled him onto his back. His face was red and he was still trying to breathe as I sat on his meaty pecs, one knee on either side of his head, grabbed him by the hair, and pulled his head into my crotch, rubbing my cock over his face. "Yeah, you want to suck that big dick, don't you, bitch?"

"Fuck...*you!*"

I jumped to my feet and stomped on his steel abs. He doubled up, gasping and choking. I jumped onto them with both feet, and that was when I noticed his cock was hard.

It was a beautiful cock, long and thick over a set of heavy balls. He had trimmed his golden pubic hair to fuzz. I reached down and flicked his cock with my right index finger. "Looks like getting your ass kicked turns you on too, muscle man," I said, laughing.

I had him where I wanted him now. I picked up his left leg, spun it so it was wrapped around my left leg, crossed it across his right knee and then dropped onto my ass, locking my right ankle over his left foot.

A figure four hurts like a motherfucker, and sure enough, he was screaming his submission before I could even ask him.

I released the hold and got to my feet. I kicked his left knee—the one the submission hold had tortured—and he screamed again and rolled away.

I followed him as he crawled to the corner, and as he started climbing the ropes I kicked him square in the small of his back. He dropped down to his knees, and I planted my right foot in between his shoulder blades while grabbing both wrists and yanking his arms back.

"What do you say, muscles?" I asked. My cock was getting harder. Every muscle in his back strained as he tried to power out of the hold. But no one is that strong—the leverage I had was too much even for someone as powerful as Max Coleman. His asscheeks clenched as he struggled, and I knew when he submitted this time he was going to pay for everything.

"I submit! God, I submit!"

"What did you say?" I asked.

"I SUBMIT! I SUBMIT! I SUBMIT!"

I let him go, and he leaned against the ropes. I stuck my right index finger in my mouth and licked it. I pressed up against him, putting my mouth to his ear. "I'm going to fuck you, bitch."

"No, man, no!"

I slid my slick finger into his asshole. He resisted until I slipped my left arm around his thick neck, my forearm flexing against his head, and yanked backward. His ass relaxed and my finger slid in. A moan escaped his lips.

"Yeah, you know you want it." I stood up, maintaining my hold on his neck so he had to come up with me. I pulled my finger out of his asshole, reached into my boot and pulled out the condom I'd tucked there earlier. I tore the package open, spit into it, and slid it one-handed over my cock. I tightened my arm around his neck and pulled him onto his toes, then kicked his legs apart, sliding the tip of my cock inside his hole.

His body stiffened, every hard muscle tensed even harder, then he relaxed with a shudder.

"You want the whole thing, don't you?"

"Yes," he whimpered.

I shoved my stiff cock inside him.

He screamed—but the scream died into a primal growl.

He arched his back and shoved his ass toward me.

"Give it to me!" he snarled in his deep, masculine voice.

Oh, hell yeah. There's nothing hotter than a massive muscle stud who not only likes to get fucked—but who wants it hard.

I slapped his bubble butt and slid slowly out until all that was left inside was the head of my engorged cock. He writhed, his pumped muscles trembling with desire. He tried to push back, to force my cock back in, but I grabbed his right arm and twisted it behind him. I leaned forward and whispered into his ear. "Beg for it."

"You *bastard*." He spit the words out. Still gripping his arm, I released my choke hold and grabbed his cock with my left hand. He moaned as I stroked him. We stood, the tip of my cock inside his ass...and then, as I sensed his orgasm starting to build, I rammed deep into him, thrusting hard, up on my toes. He rose up onto his toes with a loud moan, and he came...and I pulled back and started pushing into him harder and faster until I could feel my come starting to rise, until I shot my entire load, my head going back and a gasping growl tearing out of me.

We froze like that for I don't know how long, his sweat-soaked body and mine joined.

I dropped his arm and pulled out of him, peeling off the condom and tossing it into the garbage can outside of the ring.

He turned around and smiled at me.

Warily, I took a step backward.

He grabbed me and pulled me into a big hug, crushing me in his big arms. He kissed my neck and whispered, "Come spend the night with me." His hands came down and cupped my ass. "I want you to tie me up, man. Please."

I smothered a laugh and kissed him. "I'd love to."

"That was *hot*, guys," the Boss called out. "Nice job."

"Come on," Max said, winking at me. "Let's get in the shower—and then head to my place."

I followed him into the locker room.

THE AMBIVALENT GARDENER AND THE STATE OF GRACE

Jamie Freeman

D ouble damnation, Sherie, your husband is gorgeous." Wanda
sipped her sweet tea and stared out the kitchen window.

Sherie wiped her forehead with the back of her wrist and glanced out the window. She stopped and gritted her teeth in annoyance.

"You know that bitch Nancy has to come out and sit on that damn porch swing every time Jericho sets foot in that yard."

"Slut," Wanda hissed.

"Bitch," Sherie's voice stretched the word out like a string of summer taffy. *Bee-itch.* "And why does he have to spend so damn much time out there in the yard anyway? Planting bulbs and pruning the roses and mowing the damn grass? Why doesn't he just let me get a couple of Mexicans to come do that stuff? Maria's brother said he'd give us a good price."

"Maria's Cuban," Wanda muttered absently.

"Well, what the hell's that supposed to mean, Wanda?"

"I don't know, just that they're not Mexican, they're Cuban."

"Wanda, what difference does it make? You are so dizzy some-times, I swear and—god, just look at him out there, standing in the middle of the yard in those damn shiny shorts trimming that tree and putting on a muscle show for Nancy. That bitch."

Wanda stood beside her, shaking her head and jiggling the ice in her glass, watching Jericho stretch his body taut, imag-ining him standing naked out on the lawn, his enormous body glistening in the sunlight, every muscle tanned and gleaming. He beckoned to her with an outstretched arm and a shiver ran down the length of her back.

"You cold, honey?"

"No, it's just the ice," she said, turning away from the window and sitting back at the table. She refilled her tea from the glass pitcher, condensation dripping onto the lace tablecloth.

"I heard Nancy's fucking that black cardiologist over at the—"

"You can't call him black."

"The hell I can't."

"No, it's true; you gotta call 'em African Americans, like the president."

"Oh, lord, Sherie, don't get me started on that—"

"You really think Nancy's diddling that cardiologist?"

"Oh, I know it for a fact."

Sherie turned around, leaning against the counter and folding her wet arms across her apron. "Bullshit you know for a fact," she said.

"Hand to god," Wanda said, raising her right hand like a well-paid perjurer.

"How do you know?"

"Popeye told me—"

"Don't call him that, Wanda. His name is Pete."

"Well, he's got those big ol' muscular arms and Navy tattoos an' all—"

Sherie gave Wanda *the look* and they settled into silence for a moment.

Sherie caved first. "What did Pete tell you?"

"Well, just that he was cleaning the doctor's pool and out comes Nancy, sweet as can be and she's all peaches and cream, telling him how strong he is and what big muscles he has and all the while, taking off her bikini and walking around buck naked save for her Manolos and pouring herself a glass of ice water and asking poor Pete if he wants some and, well, you can pretty much guess what that means."

"Just because Nancy was at his house swimming in the nude—"

"Sunbathing," Wanda corrected her.

"Right, sunbathing. Just because she was at his house sunbathing nude doesn't mean anything, Wanda. Welcome to the twenty-first century."

"The way Pete was grinnin' I got the impression something was going on. You know, something romantic or whatever."

"What the hell would Pete know about women?"

Wanda looked at her, startled. "What's that supposed to mean?" she asked.

"Oh, please. Everybody knows he's a *homosexual*." Her voice dipped to a whisper, her lips twisting the word with the slithering cadences of orange blossom honey and malice.

"Well, I didn't know," Wanda said, gripping her glass more tightly. "He used to date Stephanie O'Steen."

"Clueless," Sherie snapped.

"No she's not—"

"Wanda, she got lost on the way to church last week."

"She did not."

"Dumb as a box of peach pits, that one," Sherie insisted.

"Well, I don't believe that," Wanda said, shaking her head, watching the water bead on her glass.

Sherie looked out the window to make sure her husband was still working on the lawn and then ducked down close to Wanda, touching her hand with long cool fingers. "One night a couple of weeks ago, I saw Pete watching Jericho through the window."

"*What?*" Wanda let out a little sound that was half shriek, half giggle.

"And he was jerking himself."

"What? Oh, my god, oh, my god, you are joking, Sherie!" Wanda was so excited by this image that her breath became ragged and she pressed her palm firmly against her breast.

"Nope, I swear to god." Her accent was dripping now, pulling extra syllables out of "swear" and "god," each syllable adding to her delight in recounting the story. "I was sitting in the TV room and Jericho was upstairs changing clothes after work. It was late, maybe nine-thirty or so, and it was dark outside and about five minutes after Jericho went upstairs I saw Pete walk right up to his bedroom window in nothing but a blue robe and he was looking across at our house, and he wasn't there but a minute before he'd untied that robe and let it drop open and he was..." She faltered.

Wanda urged her on in whispered exhortations. "What? What happened? What did he do then?"

Sherie dropped her voice again, glancing around the room again. "He had a hard-on, Wanda. And he started touching himself and loving on himself something fierce and about the time he...you know," she blushed at the thought of saying it, but she pressed on. "It was about that time I realized he wasn't watching me at all, he was looking in the window of the upstairs bedroom."

"You thought he was watching you?"

"Well, of course I did, Wanda. You don't—"

"But he was looking at Jericho?"

"Yes, at Jericho, what'd I say?"

"Holy shit, Jericho'd kill the little queer."

"I know," Sherie said, "I know."

"Well, what happened?" Wanda asked, leaning forward.

"Nothing."

"What d'you mean, nothing?"

"Nothing," Sherie insisted. "I heard the shower upstairs and after a while Jericho came downstairs and I told him what happened, and he said he hadn't seen anything and maybe if I stopped watching so much garbage on television, I'd quit hallucinating fairies in the garden."

"He wasn't mad?" Wanda asked.

"He didn't believe me, not one word."

"Well, I'll be," Wanda said, biting her lip, thinking hard.

"You know, sometimes I don't know why I stay married to that man."

"Who?"

"My husband, Wanda. Can't you listen to me for five minutes without going off on one of your damn fool woolgathering expeditions?"

"Jericho's a catch, honey."

"He ain't all that," Sherie said, taking a glass off the counter and dispensing ice from the door of the refrigerator.

"He's all that and a bag o' chips!" Wanda said.

"Don't be stupid."

"I'm not stupid."

Sherie sighed. "I've been thinkin' of leaving him."

"Oh, honey. No."

"It's time. He doesn't love me anymore, and, you know.

I haven't loved him since Emory was a little boy. And there's someone else that—"

The kitchen door slammed open and Jericho barged into the room grinning and beautiful beneath a layer of sweat and dust. Wanda wanted to lick him clean. Sherie wanted to slap the grin off his face.

"Hey, Wanda," he said. "Sherie, honey, do we have any—"

"Shoes!" she shouted at him. He froze. Wanda looked up in surprise.

"What?" he said.

"Don't you come in here like that, I just cleaned the floors," Sherie said.

"Maria will be here in the morning," he said, toeing off his shoes and peeling off his sweat-soaked socks. He tossed them behind him onto the grass. He stood grinning at them, clean and perfect from the ankles down, toes wriggling against the cool tile of the kitchen floor.

"What do you want, Jerk-o," Sherie said. "Wanda and I were talking."

He winked at Wanda and padded over to the refrigerator. "I was just gonna ask if we got any Gatorade." He rooted around until he found a bottle of blue liquid and then closed the door and leaned against the counter. He tipped the cold liquid to his lips and drank it down in a long sensual movement. His shiny Gator basketball shorts were wet and loose, the head of his thick cock sliding visibly beneath the material when he moved. The waistband of the shorts rode low on his perfectly sculpted abs, a trail of dark hair emanating from beneath the elastic and scaling the mountain of muscle that became the broad outlines of his chest. Wanda stared slack-jawed and silent. Sherie scowled her hatred at him nearly as visibly as her friend radiated pink waves of desire. Jericho finished the bottle of Gatorade and looked at the two women for a moment.

"Have you seen Emory?" he asked.

"He's probably across the street buying pot from that bitch Nancy," Sherie said.

"I doubt that," Jericho said, rinsing the bottle and tossing it in the blue recycle bin.

"Oh, why is that, Jon Caleb Thomas?" she asked, underlining her scorn by spelling out his entire legal name. "Is your precious boy too good to get mixed up with the likes of Nancy?"

Jericho grinned at her and Sherie wanted to pick up a knife off the counter.

"It's not that, darlin'. I just happen to know for a fact our son buys his weed from Ted Whittaker."

"Get the hell outta my kitchen," Sherie shouted. When Jericho chuckled again Sherie threw the glass across the room, shattering it against the tile and showering the floor around Jericho's feet with shards of glass.

He turned on her, "Goddamnit, Sherie! I've had about enough of you," he bellowed. "I'm leaving for Chicago tomorrow morning; can we just call a truce for the next twelve hours?"

She stared at him, face red with anger and shame.

"Can we fuckin' do that?" he shouted, the veins in his neck bulging, his muscular chest flushing an angry mottled red and white.

She looked at him, grinned angrily and reached for Wanda's glass.

He parked his truck in the long-term lot and pulled his bag off the passenger seat. He hefted it up on his shoulder and walked across the shimmering parking lot, breaking a sweat in the hundred yards to the single terminal.

When it was time to preboard, Jericho looked up and saw

Randy making the first boarding call and then turning over the desk to the short blonde whose name he couldn't remember. Jericho flashed his boarding pass, slipping through the gate and out across the sunny tarmac.

When he got to his seat, Randy appeared out of nowhere.

"Warm nuts, Jericho?"

He laughed. "No thanks, Randy."

"You know, one of these days, you're gonna take me up on my offer," Randy said, laughing and stepping aside to let one of the coach passengers slip past him.

"You know something, Randy? One of these days, I just might." Heads turned in Jericho's direction as his baritone laugh danced through the cabin.

"Keep surprising me, Jericho," Randy said. Jericho watched his round bubble butt as he sauntered to the front of the plane. He looked like he'd been working out, especially his legs, which were growing thick and hard beneath the dark airline-issue pants.

The flight to Charlotte was quiet; Jericho listened to a random mix on his iPod, wandering through Brad Paisley, Dolly Parton, the Dixie Chicks, Reba McEntire. He and Sherie were screaming more than they were talking these days. He hadn't meant to lose his temper in front of Wanda, but when that second glass shattered on the door frame beside him, he'd lost it, screaming and carrying on like the anger ball she always accused him of being. The truth was he was pretty genial except when she pushed him—and after twenty years of marriage she knew just where his buttons were.

But it hadn't always been like that. They'd been so good in high school and college; she'd been his best friend. When he wrestled competitively in high school, she'd come to his meets, and he'd gone to see her in a string of musicals at the Gainesville Community Playhouse: *South Pacific; Hello, Dolly; Guys and Dolls.* All of it a little screechy and nonsensical to him, but he'd gone and he'd brought her flowers on her opening nights, and he'd clapped and hooted during the curtain calls, and really, he'd enjoyed it, enjoyed seeing her doing something she loved so much. And college was pretty much the same. She'd gone to the Gator games and watched him play; he'd gone to sorority fashion shows and dances and loved her so much he could barely breathe in her presence.

He had never fallen out of love with her. She was still flawlessly beautiful to him. He still sometimes looked up from his morning coffee and saw her coming down the stairs in something flowy and flouncy and he'd get a hard-on and feel his pulse start a stallion's gallop. But those moments of passion were becoming fewer and farther between and were greeted by Sherie with silence or sarcasm. The last time he'd tried to kiss her, maybe a month or two ago, she'd pulled away and told him to go take a fuckin' cold shower.

He couldn't think of anything to say in response; he'd just walked out onto the deck, stripped off his shirt and shorts and lain naked in one of the lawn chairs that faced the pool, eyes closed against the world and the setting sun.

He suspected she was having an affair with Jerry Hopewell, the minister at the church they sporadically attended. About five years ago Sherie had been born again, a concept that seemed a little alien to Jericho, a little un-Methodist, really, but that's how she characterized her experience: born again. As if somehow her poor mother had botched it the first time. She had suddenly become a member of every class and committee, dragging poor hapless Wanda along with her. Overseeing all this passionate activity was the dashing (married) figure of Jerry Hopewell, former runway model and Methodist minister extraordinaire.

Jericho and Emory had been skeptical. Emory flat out told

his mother that he was fourteen and an atheist, and he was not going to church. Jericho was ambivalent about religion, as he was about so many other things, and had agreed to accompany her to Sunday services periodically, but had disappointed her with his lack of religious fervor.

And in the midst of his wife's spiritual transformation, something happened to Jericho as well, something that jolted him like a bolt of heaven-sent lightning.

It was around Easter, the spring after Sherie's conversion, and Jericho had been out back by the pool, planting geraniums in the giant terra-cotta planters that ringed the far side of the patio. He had his hands deep in the potting soil when he heard Sherie clicking across the flagstones, her annoyance somehow clear in the rhythm of her steps. He looked up at her, shielding his eyes from the sun, and realized there was a man he did not recognize standing beside her.

"This is the pool guy," she said, then, "I'm going to the church picnic; I guess you don't have time to celebrate the rebirth of the Lord."

"Not at the moment, no," he said, standing.

He and the pool guy watched her click back in the direction of the house.

"Holy shit," the pool guy said.

"Yeah, she's something else, ain't she?" Jericho said.

"At least," the pool guy said.

"I'm Jericho," he extended a hand.

"I'm Pete," the pool guy said, "the pool guy."

"You live behind us," Jericho said.

Pete nodded. "Yeah, I own Petrovsky Pools. We do most of the pools in the neighborhood."

Pete was over six feet tall with a broad, muscular chest that spread the cotton of his tank top thin and tight. His arms were huge, the bulging muscles inked with intertwining tattoos, tribal bands and a couple of Navy tats. His broad upper body sliced down to his hips in a thick triangle of flesh supported by strong, well-proportioned legs. His thighs bulged from his cargo shorts and his legs were covered with strawberry blond curls. His hands and feet were large but perfectly formed. He was a Norse god come to life.

When their hands touched, Jericho's face flushed, and he knew by the subtle narrowing of Pete's eyes that he recognized the color of desire on his cheeks. They stood in awkward silence for a few minutes and then Jericho walked him over to the cabana where they kept the pool supplies.

Pete had changed him, at that moment, in an uncomfortable and unexpected way, though in years to come, when he recounted this first encounter to others, he would be greeted by incredulous looks and snorts of laughter. *How could he, after all, not have realized he was gay?*

It just hadn't clicked for Jericho until Pete touched his hand that day. And then suddenly a million little moments in his past shifted into place, neat rows of seedlings sprouting before his eyes. *Oh, shit,* he thought, *holy fuck.*

He had always been a big guy, always outside with the horses, working in the fields or on his daddy's trucks, and so the natural progression from farm chores to weight lifting and competitive wrestling seemed as natural as the hair that sprouted between his legs and crawled across the muscles of his belly to the gentle slope between his pecs.

In high school, his wrestling coach started calling him Jericho, telling people "God himself couldn't make this boy come tumbling down." And for the most part that had been true. He had led his team to state championships every year. And he had loved wrestling, loved the smell of it and the feel of it. Loved the closeness of the combat and the impending exhaustion that would hit him later, when the trophy was won and the adrenaline had dissipated.

And he had missed the wrestling once he graduated high school. UF didn't have a wrestling program, but he'd managed to play football well enough in high school to leave the wrestling mat behind and run out onto Florida Field as a Gator. He had sailed through four seasons of football and come to love it as much as he'd loved wrestling. The Gators officially took the SEC Championship his junior year; they'd earned it the year before but been denied the title as a result of SEC sanctions. By 1991, Gators Coach Spurrier and the boys were riding high, and Jericho was riding with them.

He'd gotten a lot of attention from girls at UF, enough in fact, to drive Sherie to force an engagement ring from him during their sophomore year. But he'd also gotten a lot of attention from guys at UF, a fact he initially failed to recognize. He soaked up the attention of his male admirers as carelessly as a palm tree soaks up the tropical heat. Only in retrospect did he recognize the pattern twisting through his life like an invasive vine, something tropical, yes, but lazy and heady too, something that flowered at inopportune moments and then died away when the weather shifted.

Once on an overnight trip he'd had to share a hotel room with a guy they all called "Bakery," and he'd awakened in the middle of the night spooning Bakery's sleeping breadbasket, his erection straining beneath the cloth of his tighty-whiteys, perfectly aligned with Bakery's crack. He'd eased himself away, untangling his arms from Bakery's muscled torso. He'd heard a catch in Bakery's breath and then, in the softest, beer-soaked whisper, "It's okay, Jerk-o." But Jericho had rolled over, watching the wallpaper on the wall beside him shift from darkness into early morning light. When the digital clock on the bedside table finally read 5:30, Jericho pulled on his clothes, slipped out of the room, and ran fifteen miles through the chilly dawn.

There were other times too, moments when the vine burst into spontaneous bloom, times when he'd felt light-headed and disoriented from its seductive masculine perfume. Kissing that handsome artist, Jude, at Claire and David's house, lips touching briefly under the moonlight; watching porn with buddies in college; sleeping half naked with his work buddies, three to a bed at the hunting cabin he borrowed from his Uncle Jon; flirting wordlessly with strangers in elevators and hotel lobbies. The moments, so separate and diffused before, twisted into clear relief when his hand touched Pete's and his sexual ambivalence shifted to a startling, brilliant certainty.

These thoughts were whirling around his head as the plane approached Chicago. Brad Paisley's crooning voice comforted him and eased him into sleep.

He took a cab to the hotel, changed and headed for the office, focusing on work until the evening wound down and the final meeting dissolved into groups of men and women leaning against tables or standing in doorways talking about dinner and smelling of sweat and coffee.

Jericho tapped out the final lines of an email and shut down his laptop.

"Hey, Jerk-o, you up for a bit o' lifting?"

Jericho looked up and smiled.

"Yeah, baby," he said, tucking the laptop into his shoulder bag.

He and Josh had struck up a friendship at a corporate retreat in Arizona and eventually become workout buddies whenever Jericho came to Chicago.

They rode the elevator up to the corporate gym, which was perched on the top floor of the building with a stunning, vertiginous view of the city. They changed clothes and cycled through the weight machines, finishing up with a run, feet pounding out a steady rhythm on the treadmills, talking and watching the blinking skyline outside the windows.

"You still thinking about coming up here?" Josh asked.

"Cliff's been pushing pretty hard."

"Of course; he's scared shitless of losing you to ATR in Atlanta."

"They're a bunch of crooks and crazies."

Josh laughed. "Don't tell him that; you might need the leverage."

"Maybe," Jericho laughed. "Up?"

"Up," Josh said, increasing the incline. "I wish you'd consider it seriously. Chicago's a great city."

Jericho glanced at Josh, whose eyes were glued to the skyline.

"Yeah, maybe," he said.

"Not maybe, Jericho, it'd be good for you. You need a change."

"How do you know what I need?" Jericho asked, his voice gentle, betraying him.

"Oh, I know what you need, bubba," Josh said, eyes catching Jericho's and winking broadly.

Jericho blushed. "Up?" he said, reaching to adjust the incline again.

"Up," Josh said.

When they finally hit the showers, Jericho's body felt hot and loose and wonderful. His joints were light; his limbs rangy as a scarecrow's. He stripped off his workout clothes, grabbed a towel and walked into the tiled shower room where Josh was already lathering up under a steaming stream of water. Jericho glanced at Josh, whose muscled body was slick with soap, the runoff forming rivulets in the hair on his thighs and his chest. His nipples poked out of his chest hair, dark and heavy and succulent.

Jericho felt the warm looseness of his limbs being eclipsed by the growing tightness between his legs. He threw his towel over the low half wall and approached the showerhead closest to Josh.

He blasted the cold water and ducked his head under the stream until his body relaxed again.

"Watch it, man. You're spraying that ice water all over me."

Jericho's face emerged from the chilled spray, spitting a stream of water in Josh's direction. "What?"

"Nothing." Josh laughed. "You staying the weekend?"

"Yeah," Jericho said. "No reason to go home."

"Yikes."

"Yeah, Sherie's probably riding the reverend as we speak; she'd probably rather have me gone for good."

"Jesus, man, when you gonna put a stop to that?"

Jericho lathered his body thoughtfully, and then looked up at Josh, fingers clutching the bar of soap to his hairy chest.

His eyes met Josh's and he felt the sting of emotion in them. "We've been together for twenty years," he said softly.

"I'm sorry, man; I had no right to say that." Josh reached out and took Jericho's bulging arm in his hand, their flesh connecting awkwardly beneath the rush of water. They stood still, eyes locked for a long time.

"Is there anything I can do?" Josh said finally.

Jericho stepped forward, his body moving slowly, as if his muscles had suddenly turned to stone. He leaned forward and Josh leaned toward him. Their lips met, just as a voice cried out in startled anxiety.

"*Ay, dios mio. Lo siento, Señores. Lo siento!*" The cleaning woman wheeled her cart back down the hallway, shouting out a litany of apologies.

Jericho laughed. Josh grabbed him and pulled him against his chest and kissed him fiercely. Jericho felt dizzy with arousal. He pulled back, grabbing Josh's arms and pushing him away. They stood like this for a long time, bodies frozen, eyes uncertain.

"I'm sorry," Josh said.

"No, no," Jericho said.

"Jericho, it's okay; I know you're married. I'm really sorry, man. That was, well, what wasn't supposed to happen."

Jericho was dizzy. He was falling through the branches of his old life, plummeting uncontrollably toward the earth below. He reached out to steady himself against the firm, warm tile.

Josh looked startled.

"What should we do this weekend?" Jericho asked finally, reaching over to turn off the water.

Josh, relieved but puzzled, said, "How would you feel about a cowboy-themed circuit party?"

"I have no fuckin' clue what that means," Jericho said, reaching for his towel.

By seven o'clock Friday evening, Jericho had worried himself into a state of near panic. He paced, then checked his emails, then paced, then changed his shirt, then paced some more. He had called Sherie, but her cell phone was turned off. He had called Emory and talked to him for half an hour, shooting the shit about his classes and his girlfriend, Kim, and finally Emory had said, "You know she's gone, Dad."

Just like that, the words tumbling so easily from his son's lips.

"I know, Tiger," he'd said, but he had been surprised. He'd

seen it coming, but to hear it from his boy brought a wash of sadness up from his stomach. Although Emory was now nineteen, Jericho could hear the four-year-old Emory in his mind, voice high and mournful. *You know she's gone, Dad.* Goose pimples spread across his arms. He felt a cold, overwhelming sadness grip his heart, a giant fist curled angrily inside his rib cage.

"Are you okay, Dad?"

"I'm fine, Em, I just..." His voice trailed off.

"Dad, you deserve better than her."

"Emory, she's still your mother. Show some respect."

"Bullshit, Dad. She's fucking that minister; you don't deserve that."

"Emory." Jericho's lips barely formed the single word. There was a long silence. Jericho could hear music in the background on Emory's end, an old song: Ty Herndon singing "In the Arms of the One Who Loves Me." Jericho fell to his knees on the thick carpet as saliva churned in his mouth.

"Hang on a sec," he said, dropping the phone and lumbering into the bathroom. He vomited, washed his face and went back to the phone.

"Dad? Oh, my god, Dad. Are you okay? Do you want me to come to Chicago?"

"No, Tiger. I just need to chew on this for a while."

There was a long pause. "You sure?"

"I'm gonna go out with my workout buddy and get trashed and probably regret it in the morning, and then when I get home Monday, we'll figure out what to do next. Okay?"

Emory sounded relieved.

"Okay," he said.

"All right, good night, kiddo."

"Good night, Dad. I love you."

"I love you more."

Jericho clicked off the phone and tossed it on the bed, walking to the window and opening the curtains to reveal the twilight cityscape beginning to sparkle with great swathes of light.

"Is that what you're wearing?" Josh asked when Jericho opened the door.

"What?" He looked down at his jeans, cowboy boots, and long-sleeved, pearl-buttoned shirt.

Josh laughed. "It's a circuit party, not a rodeo. Here. Put this on." He tossed a wad of black cloth at Jericho. "But first, give me one of those beers. I've obviously got some catching up to do."

Jericho handed him a beer and unbuttoned his shirt. He dropped it on the back of a chair and pulled on the thin black cotton tank top. ROUGH RIDER was emblazoned across the front below the silhouette of a cowboy on a bucking bronco. Jericho looked at Josh uncertainly. Josh's tank top was white with the black silhouette of a bucking horse on the front underscored with the word HOSS.

"Come on. Trust me on this one," Josh said, leaning back in his chair and piling his boots on the coffee table.

Jericho shrugged and finished off his beer.

Josh took a long pull of his own beer, eyes glowing in the half light, wet lips glistening.

"Much better, Jericho."

Jericho walked over to him and pulled him up roughly from his chair. He wrapped his arms around Josh and kissed him like the world had just ended.

"You're sure this looks okay?" Jericho asked in the elevator.

Josh's eyes were wide and dark, almost all pupil despite the overhead fluorescents.

"You look great," he said. "Really."

The elevator doors opened on twenty and the first of the cowboys joined them. By the time the elevator reached the mezzanine, the tiny space was packed with muscular men, some in tank tops and jeans, some shirtless in jeans and boots, some in jocks and boots. They could hear the music pounding up through the elevator shaft somewhere around the sixth floor, and by the time they stumbled out into the elevator lobby the music was deafening. Josh grabbed Jericho's hand and led him to the escalator. They crowded onto a step together, Jericho sliding his arm around Josh's waist to steady them and to reassure himself.

The ornate nineteenth-century lobby of the Palmer House had been transformed into a huge dance floor that pulsed and writhed with men. Huge video screens had been mounted high in the room and a thunderous storm of light and sound flooded the enormous space. As they descended, a roar rose up from the crowd and Josh pointed to the nearest video screen. A carnival sideshow appeared on the screen and then the face of Dolly Parton drew another roar from the crowd that shook the crystal chandeliers. When the music started, the crowd shifted into whirling overdrive as a dance mix of "You Better Get To Livin'" blasted from the speakers.

As they stepped off the escalator, the crowd pushed them together, chests sliding against each other while they moved toward the center of the room. Josh held Jericho's hand high above the crowd and they danced out into the churning sea of men and muscle. The air was damp and thick with the smells of cologne and sweat and beer and poppers.

They danced close, their bodies grinding against each other, their erections sliding together through the denim. The DJ cycled through a series of country divas, the crowd roaring its approval, booming male voices joining Reba and Shania and Faith in song. They danced until they were soaked in sweat, Josh finally pulling Jericho through the crowd to the nearest bar. He ordered beers, and they made their way around the edge of the crowd as a male voice boomed out across the dance floor. Brad Paisley singing "I'm Still a Guy."

Josh pulled Jericho up a flight of stairs and they found a place to stand on one of the balconies that overlooked the dance floor. Jericho was mesmerized by the sea of male flesh undulating below him.

"Mind blowing, isn't it?" Josh asked.

"I've never seen anything like this before."

"I'm Still a Guy" segued into "Mr. Policeman." More Paisley.

"Shit," Jericho grinned. "I can't fuckin' believe this."

When they returned to the dance floor, the room was pulsing with a pounding rhythm that knocked against Jericho's chest like a rubber hammer. Dolly was belting out a thumping dance mix of "Peace Train" and the lights in the room swirled in a tumbling, spinning pattern that made it feel like the room itself was turning. All around him men danced close, their arms lifted in the air, hands moving in the waves of light and sound. *Peace train, peace train.* A white light suddenly plummeted down on them from directly above. They danced in the halogen spot, their bodies bleached pale, their clothes glowing in the light. Jericho's eyes, so full of light and energy, were momentarily blinded. He reached out, his fingers finding Josh and pulling him closer. They danced against each other, Jericho's heart filled to the brim with joy and possibility as their bodies were lifted by the music, rising above the dance floor, then above the heads of the other dancers until he and Josh had ascended into the perfect illumination of the spotlight, Dolly's voice coaxing them higher and higher, their bodies spinning and their spirits touching in a moment of perfect grace.

They danced and drank for hours. Jericho felt an unerringly beautiful sense of connection to Josh, to the lights and the music and to the men around him. He felt the peace of decision and purpose flowing through him. This was the life he had been missing and this was the life he would claim for himself. He had tended a withering garden for far too long; it was time to relinquish his past and step into this place, this shifting world of men and rhythm and light.

The Dixie Chicks were blasting out "Sin Wagon" when Josh threw his arms around Jericho's neck and leaned close. "Cowboy, take me away," he shouted. Jericho grabbed Josh's ass with both hands, wrapping Josh's powerful legs around his waist, and lifting him up off the ground. He pulled their massive chests together and whirled them around, staggering through the crowd toward the escalator.

They made out in the elevator and stumbled down the hallway.

In the silence of the room, Jericho sobered somewhat, his cock thumping out an insistent tattoo against the inside of his jeans.

He pulled Josh's shirt up across the damp hair of his chest. His pecs and flawlessly defined abs glistened with a sheen of sweat, the neatly trimmed hair bristling roughly against Jericho's fingertips. Josh's nipples, coaxed to steely attention by the cool air of Jericho's room, stood out hard and heavy from his chest. Jericho leaned down to take the left one between his teeth, biting gently, then with increasing pressure, Josh's gasps urging him on. He slid his face across Josh's chest, dragging his stubble and then his tongue against the soft flesh. He pulled back and reached for the button fly of Josh's jeans.

"Are you gonna fuck me, Jericho?" Josh's voice was gravelly and harsh.

"I'm gonna fuck you until one of us collapses." Jericho said, pushing Josh's jeans down and sliding his palm across the hot erection.

They wrestled out of their clothes. Jericho flipped Josh onto his back on the bed. He stepped between his legs and pushed Josh's feet up, pulling the backs of his thighs against Jericho's chest. He licked his thumb and then rubbed it along the ridge between Josh's asscheeks, toying with the soft pucker and then sliding slowly inside. Josh moved against him, his eyes becoming dark slits, his breathing becoming deeper, more ragged.

When Josh was lubed up, Jericho tore open a foil packet with his teeth and rolled a condom onto his thick cock. He pushed the head against Josh and in a moment, he was inside. The heat of this first-time fuck startled him, and he pulled back, then pushed harder, thrusting himself inside Josh until his cock was buried to the base. Josh gasped before coaxing Jericho deeper, moaning and rocking his massive body back and forth, his muscles flexing, and Jericho had to look away to keep himself from coming right then.

He pushed Josh's legs apart, wrapping them around his waist and leaning forward to bite his right nipple. Josh jerked, his ass muscles tightening around Jericho's cock. They both gasped.

"I like that," Josh whispered.

"I guess I do, too," Jericho said, sliding the stubble on his chin against the sensitive pink flesh and increasing the rhythm of his fucking.

They moved together, the power behind Jericho's pistoning cock building slowly until neither could resist.

"I'm gonna come," Josh gasped.

"Come on, baby." The words had barely left his lips when

Josh let loose a huge spurting explosion of come that flew past his head toward the headboard, and then rained down on his face, his chest and his stomach. Jericho pulled out, yanked off the condom, pushed Josh's legs forward and pumped his own come onto Josh's hairy ass, sliding the head of his cock through the rough curls and leaving a thick trail. Jericho dropped forward on the bed, bracing himself on his muscular arms, letting Josh's legs drop down around his waist. Their hard stomachs pressed together, the come squelching between them. Jericho pushed up on his arms and then bent down, kissing Josh fiercely until his arms, becoming increasingly shaky as the orgasm sapped the strength from them, finally collapsed, dropping Jericho on top of Josh, every muscle trembling with exhaustion.

They slid onto their sides and drifted off to sleep, the come sliding down their skin, unnoticed.

On the flight back to Atlanta, Jericho sank into his seat and plugged into his iPod, the thumping dance rhythms clearly audible to those around him. He slipped in and out of sleep, dreams and daydreams mixing in a surreal narrative that swirled inside his head. He was going to take the job in Chicago. Maybe things would work out with Pete or Josh or maybe something else would happen. Jericho dreamed of the future for the first time in years.

He spent the first hour of his Atlanta layover sitting in a bar, drinking Wild Turkey and answering emails.

"Hello, Jericho. Can I interest you in some hot nuts?"

Jericho looked up from the table. "Randy," he said. "I'm gonna have to take you up on that offer—"

"I know," Randy said, sliding his hand absently down his muscular thigh. "One of these days."

"I was gonna say, I'm gonna have to take you up on that offer this time."

Randy stared and then laughed and said, "Well, come on. I know a place we can be alone."

During one of their more vicious fights, Sherie had shouted at Jericho that if he had spent half as much time tending her garden as he had spent tending the roses in the front yard, they'd still have a viable marriage. In retrospect, she was dead wrong. If he had spent more time tending his *own* garden they might never have married in the first place.

Before he boarded the flight from Atlanta to Gainesville, Jericho fucked Randy in a tiny storeroom, pushing into him from behind and holding their bodies together, one enormous hand resting against Randy's rock-hard abs, the other covering his mouth to muffle the groans. They had pounded into one another until Randy bit into Jericho's fingers and came all over a pile of cardboard boxes.

When he boarded the flight, he found a bowl of warm nuts on the tray table next to his seat. He grinned and popped his earbuds into his ears, letting the music ease him through takeoff.

"Look at your dad out there posing for Nancy." Pete took a swig of his beer and stared out the kitchen window, grinning.

Emory wiped his forehead with the back of his wrist and glanced out the window. He laughed. "What a fuckin' show-off."

"Well, Nancy's practically begging him for more."

"She's a flirt."

"She's a cougar. *You* better watch out."

Emory laughed again. "Oh, come on, Pete, Mama said she was having an affair with Dr. Everett."

"Wrong again."

"What?"

"Sean Everett's gay."

"Really?" Emory said, picking up a stack of dishes and taking them over to the table.

"Really gay," Pete said, dreamily.

"TMI, dude."

Pete laughed and joined Emory at the table, picking up a stack of newspapers and beginning to wrap the jumble of mugs, glasses, and plates.

"I think Carlos is gonna take care of Dad's garden while he's gone."

"Is that Maria's brother?"

"Yeah, he's got some kind of, like, agronomy degree or something and he's doing lawns until a teaching position opens at UF. Something like that; anyway, he gave Dad a good price and I think he'll pay anything to keep me from killing his precious plants."

"You think he'll be happy in Chicago?"

Emory looked up from his work. "Maybe," he said, biting his bottom lip. His eyes were glazed, distant. They sat in silence for a long time.

Pete watched Emory's face. He could see Jericho in the young man's features, a handsome, rugged genetic legacy that had evolved into this delicate, doe-eyed beauty.

"I think something happened in Chi-town," he said at last. "Something good."

"Whadda ya mean?"

Emory dragged his eyes back to Pete. "He said he had an epiphany. I don't know. He wouldn't tell me the details, but...he came back changed. For the better, I think. Something besides Mom leaving. Which is good." He nodded to himself, glancing down at his hands. "I just want him to be happy."

Pete slid his finger around the rim of a Star Trek glass, his eyebrows knitted and pensive. "I think he's gonna be fine up there," he said.

Emory looked at Pete.

"You know something," he said.

Pete tried for surprise, but blue eyes gave him away.

"What?" Emory asked.

"Nothing, I–"

"You know something, Pete. C'mon."

The kitchen door slammed open and Jericho barged into the room grinning and beautiful beneath a layer of sweat and dust. Pete looked up, a guilty smile sliding across his lips. Emory, startled, knocked an old beer glass onto the tile floor. The glass shattered.

"Shit," Emory said, starting to stand.

"No, I've got shoes on," Jericho said, reaching for a broom. "What were you two talking about, all serious like?" he asked.

Pete watched him move back and forth, beautiful muscles flexing, hefty cock swinging low and loose inside the folds of his basketball shorts. He grinned.

"Oh, my god," Emory said suddenly.

They both looked at him, startled.

"Are you two, um, you know, involved?" he said, a blush rising up his neck and spreading across his pale cheeks.

"What makes you think that?" Jericho asked.

He pointed at Pete. "The look on his face just now, and the way you look at each other when you think I'm not watching."

"Emory, it's more complicated than that."

"No, Dad. It's that simple. Good for you. Whatever. Be gay; be happy."

Pete and Jericho stared at him in silence.

Emory looked up at Jericho. "Dad, all I've ever wanted is for you to be happy."

Jericho stared at his son and felt himself crumble, bricks falling away from him like autumn leaves.

script/edits: Dale Lazarov
pencils/inks: Bastian Jonsson
shading/tones: Yann Duminil

After Hours

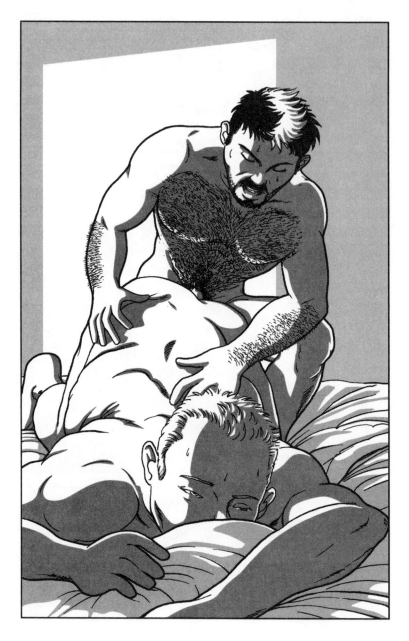

End

BRUTE

Jonathan Asche

He had a mean right hook. He sucked an even meaner cock.

I had stopped at Dot's Café in Brute, Texas, a town so far out in the middle of nowhere that time had forgotten it. It looked like everyone else had, too. There were only two other patrons at Dot's that afternoon. "Lucky I missed the lunch rush," I told the waitress. She didn't smile.

Then they walked in, three guys in blue-gray uniforms, darkened here and there with grease stains. They took the booth across from mine, nodding toward me as they sat down. Two of the guys were almost forgettable on sight, one scrawny and middle-aged, the other a doughy thirtysomething. Guy Number 3, he made an impression: a stunning muscle hunk whose brawny physique threatened to burst through his uniform shirt. It looked like his biceps already had; the sleeves were cut off just below the shoulder. Thick trapezius muscles rose out of his collar and crawled up his neck. His chest was broad; his shirt was unbuttoned just enough to give me a glimpse of golden hair, a shade darker than that curling beneath his cap, sprouting between his meaty pecs. TRAVIS was embroidered on his shirt pocket.

"Hey, pardner, how's it goin'?" the middle-aged guy asked. His shirt pocket read DALE.

"Doing okay," I said, turning my attention back to my Blue Plate Special.

"Where you from?"

Great, he wants to chat. I said: "Atlanta. Driving to Phoenix to visit my mother."

"At-*lan*-ta," repeated Dale, a crooked smile coming to his weathered face. "Ain't nothin' but coons and queers up there. Which one're you?"

The doughy guy—I didn't get a good look at the name on his shirt—guffawed like that was the funniest thing he'd ever heard.

I said, "Well, I'm obviously not black."

End of conversation.

But it wasn't the end of the talking. Dale and his tubby friend began talking loudly about what "they" ought to do "with them nasty faggots." Travis said nothing but chuckled at their hateful jokes.

I left a ten-dollar bill for my six-dollar meal and stood up, too disgusted to eat. As I left the middle-aged fuck said in a sneering falsetto, *"Toodle-oo, big boy."*

Stopping at the door I said in a soft, lisping purr: "Oh, boys."

The men were still chuckling when they looked at me. I raised my hands, middle fingers extended. "Suck my dick!"

I was at my car when Travis, the muscle hunk, charged out of the restaurant to teach me a lesson. I should've known: I could've kicked the other two hillbillies' asses with no problem, but Travis was in a higher weight class than me.

I wanted to be twenty miles down the highway before he swung the first punch, but he grabbed my arm before I could get behind the wheel. "*Wait!*"

It was his pleading tone of voice more than his grip that made me stop. When I turned to face him I was confronted by two puppy-dog eyes. He *was* pleading.

"That's true?" he asked. "You *are* queer?"

"What's it to you?"

"I'm... I'm a..." Travis looked over his shoulder, to make sure no one else was around. "I'm like you."

My eyebrows shot up my forehead. "Really?"

"Do you have to leave today?"

That made me laugh. "I want to leave right now."

"There's a motel up the road, the Maverick Inn, 'bout ten miles outside Brute. I can meet you there tonight."

I didn't answer right away. My eyes dropped down for another quick scan of his magnificent body: the flat stomach, the narrow waist, the meaty biceps, that provocative bulge at the front of his blue-gray chinos.

"How will you know what room?" I asked.

"Don't worry, I'll find you." Then: "I'm gonna have to hit you now."

"*What?*"

"They're watchin'. I gotta do *somethin'.*"

"You could just go back inside."

"Don't worry," Travis said. "I won't hit you hard."

I was doubled over gasping for breath before I could protest further. *Bull*shit, *you won't hit me hard.* When I was able to stand upright I didn't have to look at the café's front window to see Dale and his doughy buddy laughing at me; I could hear them through the glass.

* * *

It was after ten at night when Travis knocked on my door at the Maverick. He didn't have to look too hard to find me: there were only two cars in the parking lot when I checked in, and one of them belonged to the old lady at the front desk.

Travis greeted me with a sheepish grin. I should've greeted him with a fist to the face, just like I should've kept driving when I got to the Maverick Inn. But then I'd think of Travis's buff bod and all the fun I could have with it, and before I knew it I was paying forty dollars to stay in a room that belonged in a Hitchcock movie. My cock didn't hold a grudge.

He stepped inside, his he-man body seeming so much larger in the small room. He wore a black-and-white tank and a pair of blue jeans that advertised his crotch and ass like a neon sign. My crotch was doing some advertising, too, the way my cock poked at the front of my red gym shorts.

I hooked two fingers in the waist of Travis's jeans and pulled him closer. "You're overdressed," I said.

Before I could start pulling his clothes off Travis wrapped me in his thick arms and kissed me. I tasted mint as his tongue slid into my mouth. His hands glided down my bare back, burrowing beneath the waistband of my shorts and gripping my ass.

My lips were almost sore when our mouths parted. I felt dazed, perhaps because all the blood in my body had rushed to my aching cock. Travis's eyes glimmered with excitement.

I said, "I'm Heath, by the way."

He chuckled. "I'm—"

"Travis," I interrupted. "I saw your name tag earlier. Now get out of those clothes."

The tank came off first. In one swift move Travis unveiled a flawless torso, girded with voluptuous muscles. The golden hair accentuating the cleft of his beefy pecs disappeared beneath his

sternum, reappearing below his belly button and marching downward between abs you could sharpen knives on until it disappeared
beneath his jeans. My eyes followed that furry trail all the way.

"Very nice," I whispered. My hard-on seconded that opinion
with an impatient push against my shorts.

Travis unhooked the top button of his jeans. "Wait," I said.
"Turn around. Show me that ass."

The sheepish smile returned to Travis's face as he did as he
was told. With his back to me he unzipped his fly and was about
to step out of his pants when I stopped him. "Take them off
slow, like a stripper," I commanded. "Just the jeans, not the
underwear."

I could tell he felt silly, but he obeyed, revealing his perfect
bubble butt a few agonizing inches at a time. By the time his
jeans slid past the lower third of his cheeks I had decided that
my face was going to spend a good part of the night buried
between those plush, round globes. I kneaded my cock through
my gym shorts, eager to get started.

"Now take off the underwear."

He hooked his thumbs in the elastic waist of his simple white
briefs and started to pull them down in the same teasingly slow
fashion he'd removed his jeans. I waited, determined to pounce
the moment his ass was bare. Travis revealed a few inches of
asscrack and then…

Travis turned to face me, grinning proudly at his sudden
improvisation. I immediately put my plans for Travis's ass on
hold. He not only had a flawless ass, he was hung, too. His cock
was barely contained in his briefs, the thick shaft curving over
his right leg, the cockhead peeking over the waistband. Now all
I could think about was sucking that huge tool until sunrise.

I waited anxiously for Travis to pull those briefs down. It
was a wonder my tongue wasn't hanging out of my mouth like a

bloodhound's, drooling all over the floor. My cock was certainly drooling, the front of my shorts darkening as precum soaked through the fabric. It drooled even more when Travis finally pushed those white briefs down his trunklike thighs and his stiff dick sprang free.

"You're well built all over," I chuckled, wrapping a hand around his thick, cut cock. "I don't know where to start, the front or the back."

Travis said, "I'll start for you." He'd barely completed the sentence before he was on his knees and my shorts were around my ankles.

"Wait, I..." A rush of pleasure stifled my objection as Travis swallowed my throbbing cock whole.

Travis may have been in the closet, but he sure as hell wasn't a virgin. He sucked dick like a pro. His tongue delicately circled the corona of my cock and then he took the entire shaft down his throat until his lips were at the base. Just when I thought I might be getting close to coming he pulled his mouth away and went to work on my balls, cupping them in his big hands and bringing the engorged spheres to his lips to lick and suck.

"You've got a great cock," Travis whispered, rubbing it against his cheek. He looked up at me. "You've got a great *everything.*"

Travis closed his mouth over my cock once again and I was immediately dizzy from pleasure. I steadied myself on his massive shoulders while he gulped my dick down his throat. I was getting so close, but when I told him so Travis didn't ease up; he sucked my cock harder.

I came suddenly and quickly. I closed my eyes and my body jerked as my cock exploded in Travis's mouth. When I opened my eyes I saw Travis once again rubbing my dick across his face, this time leaving a sticky-slimy trail of his spit and my jism. He squeezed the base of the shaft and a heavy drop of cum oozed out the piss-slit. He snapped it up with his tongue like a frog catching a fly. Travis smiled up at me as he swallowed that bead of jizz.

I shook my head disbelievingly. "You're incredible."

"And you're hot," he said, standing. "You make up your mind, front or back?"

His cock was pulsing and a long, syrupy strand of precum hung from the head. Much as I wanted that ass I had to get a taste of that monster between his legs.

I guided him over to the bed and told him to sit. Kneeling on the floor between his legs I gripped his hard cock and licked the head, drinking up the mildly salty juice that seeped out of it. My tongue moved along the ridge beneath his plump cockhead and then traced the turgid veins of the shaft until I reached his balls.

Travis sucked in his breath. "Oh, yes," he sighed, placing a hand on my head, running it over my bristly buzz cut.

I took his cock all the way down my gullet. Travis wasn't a groaner but he was breathing hard and sometimes a moan would escape—a soft, whispery moan that was kind of cute coming from such a large man.

Then the moans got louder. Travis put both hands on my head, holding me still while he fucked my mouth. He began to make sounds that were supposed to be words but came out as hard, gasping breaths. Words weren't necessary. I knew what he was trying to tell me and readied for his load.

His body shuddered and he came in my mouth. It was thick, tangy and plentiful. I pulled my mouth away from his cock in time to get a splat in the face and then another. I put his dick back in my mouth and sucked out the last drops.

Travis helped me to my feet then pulled me to the bed. I

climbed on top of him and he drew an index finger across my chin, wiping off a gooey dollop of jizz that hung in my beard. I guided that finger between my lips, smiling as I sucked it clean.

And then we kissed for a very long time.

When our mouths finally separated, Travis asked, "Ready for the back now?"

"I'm not sure I'm done with the front yet," I said, moving down to bite one of his pert nipples. I let a hand glide down his rigid torso. "How long have you been working out to get a body like this?"

"Don't work out so much as just *work*," he said. "But I've got some weights at home. Lift 'bout four times a week. Been liftin' since high school, when I thought I'd be playing for the Cowboys."

I nodded. There were other questions I could've asked, like why did he stay in this godforsaken town. Instead my hand continued south until I reached his dick. He still had a semi. "*This* is strictly genetic," I said, gently stroking his cock.

I quickly kissed my way down to his cock, giving that meaty tool the wettest, sloppiest kiss of all. Travis inhaled sharply as I took his sensitive prick into my mouth. This time I took it slow, wanting to savor every inch—the taste, the feel of that cock as it slid down my throat. It quickly swelled in my mouth, ready for round two.

My mouth moved to his balls, resting heavily between his open legs in their velvety sac. Travis let out one of his soft moans as I prodded his golf ball–sized nuts. He spread his legs wider as my mouth traveled deeper between them, my tongue tickling the outer edges of his asshole.

Travis drew his legs up slightly, put his hands on top of my head and pushed me into that musky divide. My tongue found his sphincter and prodded the smooth ass-lips. He moaned and his asshole pulsed. When I pushed past the taut ring and into his chute Travis cried out loudly enough to be heard in the neighboring rooms if they were occupied.

His outburst was very satisfying and I felt like I had won something. I had, I supposed: his ass. But I wasn't ready to declare victory yet—not until I had him crying like a baby.

Sitting up on my haunches I ordered Travis to roll over and get his ass up in the air. He happily complied. I moved to the foot of the bed and got behind the closeted muscleman. Just looking at his naked butt took my breath away: globes of solid muscle, rising into the air like two pale hills. A few fine golden hairs curled out of the cleft of his buttocks, beckoning me to hunt the treasure buried within. I brought my hands down onto Travis's buttcheeks and ordered him to spread his legs wider until that treasure was exposed. His asshole was more like a pair of light pink, primly drawn lips than a rosebud, even when it knotted into a pucker.

I wet one of my thumbs in my mouth and rubbed it across those pink asslips. Travis's sphincter throbbed at my touch. Using both my thumbs I pried those pink lips apart, revealing a darker pink inside. I gently stroked the opening, smiling as Travis let out another one of his breathy moans. His hips gyrated, grooving to my touch.

That's when I dived in, plunging my face between those hills of muscle, my tongue spearing his asshole.

There were no soft moans this time. A shriek burst from Travis's lips before he buried his face in a pillow to muffle his cries. I pushed my tongue deeper into his chute, enjoying the fight with his quivering asslips as they instinctively tried to shut me out. Travis was enjoying the fight, too, grinding his ass into my face as I tongue-fucked his hole, groaning into the pillow and seizing the Technicolor bedspread in his fists when the pleasure got too unbearable.

I tore into his ass with greater ferocity, licking and gnawing at that throbbing hole and then driving my tongue into it as far as it could go. I dragged my entire face up and down that open trench, tickling his skin with the coarse hairs of my beard. Moving down, I slurped on his balls, sucking them into my mouth and tugging on them just enough to make Travis jump. I reached between his legs and gripped his cock. It was like iron. I pulled it back toward my lips, swabbing away the silvery string of precum that hung from the piss-slit like tinsel on a Christmas tree.

Travis raised his head off the pillow. "Fuck me," he said, his voice hoarse.

"You really want me to?" I asked playfully, flicking my tongue against his pulsing asshole.

"Fuck me," he repeated.

I didn't make him say it a third time.

Condoms and a bottle of lube were already set out on the night table in anticipation of this moment. I grabbed a rubber and the lube and hastily prepared myself. Then I prepared Travis, squeezing a generous amount of lubricant directly onto his winking hole. I slid two fingers into that hole. His sphincter gripped my fingers below the second knuckle. I worked a third finger inside him, slowly stretching his ass-ring. My cock vibrated, anxious to follow my fingers into that hot chute.

Kneeling behind Travis, I gripped the base of my dick and pushed it against his pursed asslips. They resisted, so I pushed harder until those lips grudgingly parted. Travis let out a sharp, whimpering cry as my cock burrowed deeper into his hole. When my cock was buried in his gut all the way to the hilt, we both let out satisfied groans.

I began to pump his ass in deliberate thrusts. Each time I sank my cock into his hole I got a jolt that sizzled down the length of my rod and hummed throughout my body. I rammed him harder, sending his body forward when my pelvis hit the back of his ass.

Travis buried his face in the pillow once again, muffling his ecstatic cries. He rolled his hips, working his body in time to my driving cock. I leaned over him, the pornographic thoughts swirling in my head tumbling out of my mouth in partial grunts. Then I rose up off my knees so I was crouched over his ass in a leapfrog position. Resting my torso against his broad back, I continued fucking him, my ass bobbing wildly as I pulled my cock almost entirely out of his hole and plunged it back inside.

Travis and I quickly became a sweaty, slobbering, writhing mass. Anyone passing by the motel room door would swear a grizzly and gorilla were wrestling inside. That assumption wouldn't be too far from the truth. We were animals acting on raw, primal desire. It was the best kind of sex, when you let go of all social pretenses and let your cock take control.

We fell into a spoon position. Travis's dick was twitching like a divining rod at Niagara Falls. It was almost as wet as Niagara; there was a sizable wet spot on the bedspread from where his cock had been drooling its juices. I reached around Travis's waist and closed a fist around that red, swollen rod. It throbbed in my hand as I stroked it and Travis trembled against me. This big, brawny hunk was now a blubbering heap of jelly. I'd be lying if I said this didn't excite me: it was David conquering Goliath, not with a stone but with his cock.

The bed rocked like a raft on a stormy sea as Travis thrashed about, his body jerking as I jerked on his dick. He was sucking in a mouthful of air when he came, his breath catching in his throat, his body stiffening as he shot his load. It was another copious wad splattering everything—his abs, my hand, the ugly bedspread. I cried out—"Oh, *yeah!*"—cheering him on as his cock spat out the last gooey squirts of cum. I kept stroking his dick until he couldn't stand it any longer and swatted my hand away.

I could hardly stand it myself. My body was buzzing with erotic pleasure, a pleasure that increased each time I shoved my cock into the warm depths of Travis's ass. I seized one of his pecs, digging my fingers into the hard muscle and holding on as I jackhammered his hole on my final sprint toward orgasm. I didn't want to let him go and in the seconds before I came I plotted to extend our time together—I'd call my mother in Phoenix and say I had car trouble and would be delayed a couple days, days that would be spent in a shabby motel room in West Texas. I then began to plan what Travis and I would be doing in our motel room. First I'd kiss every one of those taut muscles of his, but the muscles I'd kiss the most would be his glutes—and his sphincter muscle. I wouldn't stop eating his ass until he blew his load. Then I'd say, "How 'bout a protein shake," and shoot my load down his throat and he'd look up at me and smile as he licked it off his lips. And then...

And then I came.

I didn't call my mother and Travis didn't spend the next couple of days with me. He spent the night though. I awoke with a raging hard-on pressed against his ass. He moaned as I rubbed it between his buttcheeks. I was ready to begin the day with another hot fuck, but then Travis asked what time it was. He jumped out of bed the moment he learned it was almost eight o'clock.

"I gotta be somewhere at nine," he said, dashing into the bathroom to pee.

Of course he did.

Thirty minutes later we were both stepping out of the room into the dry heat of the morning, exchanging awkward good-byes before making our respective getaways. We weren't quick enough. An old pickup truck speeding down the highway came to a stop so abruptly it almost skidded off the road. When it recovered, it made a right and came tearing across the motel's parking lot, heading right for us. I didn't have to see inside the cab to know who our visitors were.

"I thought we runned you outta town yesterday, faggot," Dale called out from the driver's side window when his truck jerked to a stop. His doughy friend giggled idiotically. "Guess ya' didn't figure on Travis catching you."

"Guess I didn't," I said.

"Go on, Travis. Make sure this cocksucker learns good and well never to bring his perverted ass back here."

Travis looked at his coworkers and then at me. His eyes were beseeching as his hands slowly curled into fists. He was going to have to hit me again.

I stepped closer to him. "You have muscles," I said, "but no strength."

I dropped my duffle bag, cupped Travis's face in my hands and kissed him hard and with plenty of tongue.

Travis's fists melted and instinctively went to my waist. Realizing his error he pulled away as if bitten by a snake. But it was too late. Dale and his fellow shithead were too stunned to speak. Travis looked to be on the verge of tears. His brawny body seemed to deflate before my very eyes.

I fished the room key out of my pocket. "Travis, be a dear and check out for me, will you?" I tossed him the key; he didn't try to catch it.

Dale and his doughy buddy started to get out the truck, but

I was in my car before they could take their hate out on me. *Don't worry, assholes*, I thought as I gunned out of the parking lot, *this cocksucker's learned never to bring his perverted ass back to Brute.*

I just hoped Travis had learned why he needed to get his perverted his ass out of it.

FIGHT CUB

Geoffrey Knight

I wasn't looking for a fight. And yet there I was, sitting in the physics end-of-year exam with a cut on my chin and a wrist so swollen that my writing hand had to drag my pen across the page like a slave with a ball and chain strapped to his ankle. Don't get me wrong, I wasn't complaining at all, because every time I stole a glance across the examination hall at Mason my cock stirred and pulsed with such pleasure I refused to stifle it. Heck, I even sat back in my chair, a different person, and let my dick harden with the memories of the night before.

But I'm getting ahead of myself.

"Get him!"

This I heard over the rattling pipes of the hot water system in the dilapidated dorm in which I lived. I'm not a member of a fraternity—I'm just not frat material. Sure, I try to look after myself, I have a pair of dumbbells stashed under my bed and when nobody's looking I do curls and dips and try not to pop a

shoulder, and to be honest with myself—which doesn't happen
all that often—my body's not that bad. Transformation from
weedy geek to lean, well-proportioned lad is definitely within
my reach. I look okay in the mirror these days—if I take off the
glasses and tousle the hair and just relax. But that's a me the
rest of the world simply never sees. Because I can't do exactly
that—I can't just relax! I'm always on my guard: woolen vests
as a shield of armor no matter what the temperature outside;
glasses for a helmet; straight, flat hair because I simply wouldn't
dare to do anything attention getting.

"*Get him!*"

The hot water was spluttering and pissing in bursts over me
as the pipes clanged and shuddered. I was the only guy in the
showers at the time. I showered late, when everyone else was
at a party or having fun at the college bar or fucking someone
in their room. It was supposed to be the safe time to take a
shower, alone, in private, with nobody to size you up and put
you down.

But suddenly I heard the cry of their voices.

I opened my eyes to the sting of soap and saw two buff guys
in ALPHA GAMMA FUCKYA T-shirts practically sliding across the
moldy tiles toward me at top speed. In their hands they held a
pillowcase, like park rangers about to bag a snake. Only *my*
snake didn't lash and hiss and spit. It simply recoiled in terror,
stunned into shrinkage, before an elbow connected with my chin
(the now gashed chin). Suddenly the white tiles all around turned
into a star-filled night sky, then swirled into complete darkness.

Physics is different from quantum physics.

Physics deals with the things we can see: an aircraft made out
of heavy metals and packed with human souls flying through
the sky; two cars bouncing off each other when they collide

while their occupants sail through the windscreen still full of momentum; an apple falling on Isaac Newton's head while he sits under a tree reading Shakespeare.

Quantum physics, on the other hand, deals with the things we can't see: what are atoms and protons and electrons and molecules and particles truly capable of? Metamorphosis? The folding of space? Time travel? What happens when you sleep? What happens when you're elbowed in the chin by a quarterback with a buzz cut and arms bigger than my thighs? Where do we really go—what alternate universes do we traverse—as minutes and hours slip by, lose their meaning, and before you know it, you're opening your eyes and your thumping head registers the fine cotton weave of the inside of a pillowcase? And the smell of manly sweat. And the sound of jocks laughing at you.

Then suddenly—

—the pillow case is whisked off your head and your flat, wet, honey hair flips and flops in the air, wanting to free itself and simply relax. But your chin is bleeding and your head is throbbing and your sight is blurred and all you can see are twenty ALPHA GAMMA FUCKYA T-shirts in front of you, all covering thick, muscled college torsos, all begging to be torn to shreds and flung to the ground.

Yes, those T-shirts would be much better off, off!

But then again, my chin was *very* sore!

"You're the money!" I heard someone say and looked up to see the gorilla-jawed, buzz-cut quarterback who had elbowed me.

I then looked down to see that I was still completely naked, my lean body glistening, having been snatched from the dorm showers. My hands were tied behind my back. I was in a rickety, broken chair in what looked like a derelict, rat-infested basement.

"Welcome to the attic," Buzz Cut screamed in my face.

Now I saw the window with its curtains drawn and the vaulted ceiling. Nobody has secret meetings in basements anymore, duh! This must have been—

"—the attic of Alpha Gamma Fuckya!" I was shouted at. "You've been chosen by the fraternity as tonight's prize!"

"Prize?" My lip cracked and started bleeding again.

"You heard me, bitch! You're here to be won."

"Won by who?" I should have said by *whom*, but I was bleeding and dizzy.

"By *whom*, bitch!" shouted Buzz Cut, surprisingly astonished by my mistake. "Jesus, it's a good thing we don't need you for your grammar skills! We need you for the end-of-year physics exam! You and your nerdy brain will be the prize for the winner of tonight's fight, and I for one intend to win. You're gonna help me pass tomorrow's test, or else!"

"Or else what?" I asked fearfully.

Buzz Cut didn't actually have an answer prepared and simply spat one out in straight rage. "Or else we'll make you wash every one of our jockstraps...with your tongue!"

He glared at me, his eyes and nostrils flaring like those of a demon from hell, but as I looked at the wall of muscled shirts in front of me all I could see were angels from heaven—in tight, torso-hugging T-shirts, with lats for wings.

I hid my increasing desire. At least that was the plan. Unfortunately my cock was less subtle. It made its way down my thigh like a plane on a runway until it took off, ascending straight up, defying both gravity and my brave intentions not to make a bad situation worse.

Buzz Cut stared at it in horror and rage, as did everyone else, including myself. "Are you listening to me, pervert! Or are you too busy having some sort of faggot fantasy!"

I gulped nervously and stammered, feeling the heat of my

erection against my belly. "N-n-neither! B-b-both! Yes! No! Shit!"

My rantings just made him madder. He was pushing the already high, tight sleeves of his T-shirt farther up his bulging biceps, true comic-strip style, and bunching up a fist, ready to beat the pleasure and desire out of me, when suddenly a piercing whistle cut the air.

It was a whistle of confidence, the sexy kind I could never make, the one that hot New York bankers in designer suits conjure up when they need a cab, with two moist fingers probing their mouths and manipulating their tongues as they blow.

Everyone ducked and covered his ears as though a missile had just passed too close overhead. Slowly the crowd of Fuckya frat boys turned then parted to reveal the one man in the room I hadn't noticed before, probably because of the wall of testosterone blocking my view.

This man—the one with the sexy whistle—was sitting at a bench press that I also hadn't noticed. He was unforgivably handsome, with a strong jaw and a flash of freckles across his perfect nose, the last sign of something innocent and sweet on his manly face. He looked to be around my age—perhaps twenty, maybe twenty-one—but his body was that of a man who'd been working out since he was a young boy. The sweat stains around his armpits and down the middle of his pecs suggested he'd just finished lifting, and now his bouldered shoulders and heaving chest looked as though they could rip their own way out of his fraternity T-shirt. Then there was the matter of his gym shorts, tight and also bulging.

Quickly I blinked away the lure of his crotch and looked once more at his face, his iceberg blue eyes, the generous locks of his raven black hair. Instantly I wanted to run my fingers through those locks, but as though reading my mind he indulged in that privilege himself, using one large hand, fingers splayed, to push bountiful strands away from his beaded forehead, raising his arm high. I could almost smell the scent of his armpit, sweet and dangerous, irresistible.

My cock thumped eagerly against my stomach, an unruly dog pawing at the door. Luckily for me nobody noticed; they were all watching the muscle-bound god, obviously their alpha male. All but one had a look of adoration on his face—Buzz Cut.

His eyes turned to hateful slits as he glared at the man on the bench press, like a tribesman who had been number two for too long. "If you think you can beat me, Mason, then bring it! I need that pass in physics and I'm ready for you!"

Mason, the god, stood. "I need to pass too, Bobby." Oh, Jesus, his voice was so calm, so confident. "And if it means getting physical over physics, I'm ready too."

Despite being slightly larger (and certainly uglier) than Mason, buzz-cut Bobby's throat clacked at the response, nervous and mad. But he stood his ground nonetheless. At least he tried. It was a difficult thing to do when Mason threw down the gauntlet by peeling off his shirt. Actually, let me do this scene justice...by replaying it in slow motion...and please forgive me if I embellish a little...but Mason didn't just peel off his shirt—he teased it off over every last inch of his torso.

First his hands crossed each other in front of his belly before hooking the hem of his body-hugging tee. His fists lifted it just a little at first, hoisting it up three inches to reveal a navel buried deep in muscle and surrounded by a trim forest of stomach hair—so much hair for a man that young, yet so under control, so beautifully clipped, so admirably well-maintained. He lifted the T-shirt higher to reveal a four-pack, then a six-pack, then a glorious *eight*-pack, because let's face it, nature smiles on some guys—as was I.

Each pack was blanketed in that neatly manicured young male's mane, a little matted in areas from sweat, twisting into inky trails here and there. He pulled the shirt higher to reveal nipples. They were small and milky brown, waiting for someone to drink them, begging for someone to suck on the trim fur around them before clenching those hard buds between his teeth.

I swallowed hard and glanced down, noticing the glimmer of precum in the eye of my tortured cock. It was a good thing that nobody was looking my way. Mason still had everyone's undivided attention...

...as he pulled the T-shirt up to fully reveal his bulking chest...

...as he tugged the shirt over his head, messing up his bouncing black locks...

...as he threw the sweaty tee on the floor and flexed his pecs.

First the left.

Then the right.

He was like a young male lion about to take charge of the pride, giving off so much intensity and testosterone I thought I was about to cum right then, right there, even with my hands tied behind my back and my legs crossed trying in vain to stifle my stiffy.

Not to be defeated before the fight even began, buzz-cut Bobby suddenly ripped—yes, literally *ripped*; apparently hot men really do that—the shirt off his wide, muscle-carved back. I'm sure I heard a telling sigh escape one of the other spectators, but everyone ignored it, much too focused now on the two subjects who began to step out a circle, turning the attic into an arena in which to fight.

The others formed a ring and included me in it so that my rickety chair became the best seat in the house, so close to the action I could smell the perspiration as Mason stepped in front of me. For a moment he stood with his back to me, sizing up the opponent opposite him. I could make out his perfectly muscled ass beneath his gym shorts, and again my cock flinched. Then suddenly he turned around, and for a heart-melting moment he smiled at me. "Don't worry, Ethan," he said, winking. "You're mine."

I gasped, completely taken aback. Instantly I wanted to know how this stranger, this god, knew my name. But all that came out of my mouth was, "Look out!"

While Mason was busy winking at me, buzz-cut Bobby charged him.

Before Mason could so much as turn, Bobby brought his fist down onto Mason's right shoulder like a sledgehammer.

A bloodthirsty cheer rose from the encircling crowd as the mighty Mason twisted and buckled under the blow, every meaty muscle in his body jolting heavily as he came down on one knee.

Swiftly Bobby followed the first blow with a left hook to Mason's jaw, striking while his opponent was still down.

Blood flew from Mason's lips as a smile spread across Bobby's.

"You sure you don't wanna quit now before I mop the floor with your pretty face?"

Mason wiped his mouth with the back of his hand and shook his head. "Fuck you."

Bobby laughed and shrugged. "You wish." This time it wasn't his fist he used; with Mason still down on one knee, buzz-cut Bobby threw a foot up into Mason's jaw as though he were kicking a football.

Mason's head flew back and his entire body contorted before folding to the floor in front of me.

As the crowd continued to chant and cheer, I stared down at the gorgeous, fallen god at my feet. Blood trickled down his chin. It had splashed onto his heaving chest and matted the hair there. Suddenly my heart ached for this battered beauty, until soon I heard myself say—beneath the noise of the frat boys but loud enough for Mason to hear—"Get up!"

Groggily Mason looked at me, strained, confused. "What did you say?"

"I said, get up! The physics lesson starts now! Newton's first law of motion states that a body is either at rest or moving in a straight line at constant velocity, otherwise known as the law of inertia."

"So?" Mason checked to see that his jaw wasn't broken.

"So get up, then get out of the way."

"What?"

"Just do it!"

My voice must have been more forceful than I realized because despite his obvious pain Mason obeyed my command without any further question or hesitation. One moment he was on his feet and back in the ring. The next, disgruntled by Mason's failure to accept defeat, buzz-cut Bobby charged at him like a bull.

Mason glanced at me, then back at Bobby. He held his ground, then a split second before impact, instead of fighting, Mason sidestepped.

Buzz-cut Bobby's momentum carried him straight into the crowd of onlookers, and with several loud grunts and groans Bobby sent himself and a group of stunned frat boys crashing to the floor.

Mason shot me a somewhat surprised and appreciative grin, licking the blood off his perfect teeth. I couldn't help but notice him steal a glance at my still stiff cock. I saw that his own crotch was beginning to bulge beneath his tight gym shorts, leaving little to my already overworked imagination. "Thanks," he said.

And there was that wink again.

Across the room, an enraged buzz-cut Bobby had pulled himself to his feet.

"Any more lessons?" Mason asked me.

"How much do you weigh?" I thought quickly.

"A hundred and ninety pounds."

"How much does he weigh?"

Mason shrugged. "Two-ten. Maybe more."

"Charge him," I said. "Don't worry, he won't use your side-step tactic. He's too stupid and far too mad."

"Are you sure?"

I nodded. "Newton's third law. To every action there is an equal and opposite reaction. The forces of two bodies on each other will direct them in the opposite direction."

"Translation?"

"Slam into the motherfucker as hard as you can and brace yourself. He's heavier. He'll fall harder."

Mason took a deep breath, took a step back, then with all the speed he could muster within the enclosed space he charged at Bobby.

Bobby grinned and accepted the challenge, running as fast as he could at Mason.

Both men dropped their shoulders low, like knights in a joust, ready for the collision. Mason held his breath as the two hulking combatants plowed headlong into each other before ricocheting apart and flying backward through the air.

Having braced for impact, Mason thudded against the floor, rolled, then seemed to bounce straight back onto his feet. Buzz-cut Bobby, on the other hand, slammed against the floor so hard that every last breath of air was knocked out of his lungs. Eyes wide, veins in his neck bulging, he wheezed and gasped desperately for oxygen.

Mason was already storming over to his flattened foe. He seized Bobby by his thick forearm and jerked him to his feet. While Bobby stood spluttering, Mason threw a punch that landed square in the middle of Bobby's face.

Buzz-cut staggered backward as the blow popped his nose open and a starburst of blood covered his face, but it also seemed to knock the air back into his lungs.

Mason quickly dealt a second blow, this time to Bobby's cheekbone. But buzz-cut seemed to absorb the strike before responding swiftly with a powerful uppercut to Mason's chin.

Stumbling unsteadily, Mason teetered backward before turning and losing his balance altogether, falling to his knees in front of me, his face landing right in my lap.

I shuddered, mortified—stunned—thrilled.

Mason simply lifted his giddy, wobbling head, his cheek brushing against my erect cock on the way up, his manly stubble rough against my silky stem. An electric shock of pure delight shot through my entire being.

"Any ideas what to do next?" was all Mason could slur, blinking back the dizziness, his mouth so close to the engorged head of my cock it were as though he was talking into a microphone. I could feel the heat of his breath—and yet Mason did not remove himself or even seem to mind at all.

"Ideas on what comes next?" I gulped. I had a pretty good guess at what the answer would be if his beautiful face stayed in my lap much longer, but Mason needed a more scientific response if he was going to win this fight. Or more accurately, win *me!*

"Force," I mumbled.

"What?"

"Newton's second law. Force equals mass times acceleration." I looked down at Mason's mighty hands and considered what those generous fists were capable of. "You have the mass, but you're pulling back on your acceleration which is in turn affecting your force index."

"What do you mean?"

"You're pulling your punches. You're aiming short. Don't aim for his face. Aim for a point *beyond* his face. Follow through. Keep up your acceleration."

At that moment, buzz-cut Bobby grabbed himself a handful of Mason's hair and yanked his head out of my lap. He spun Mason on his feet, but before Bobby could so much as curl his fist, Mason delivered a right hook like a damn freight train.

Bobby's head swiveled with the blow and a tooth rattled across the floor.

Before the buzz-cut bully could so much as register what just hit him a second fist flew at him. This time it was a hook from the left that sailed across Bobby's face, opening a gash above the eye then following through, not stopping till it was at least a foot beyond its target.

Bobby lurched backward, tried to hold himself up but tottered precariously on his quivering legs.

Mason stepped up to his opponent, pulled his right arm back, then launched it with all the power he had left in him.

Buzz-cut Bobby was unconscious before his bulky frame shook the floorboards. The entire attic went silent, I suppose wondering as I was if Buzz Cut was even still alive after that last killer blow. An unconscious snort and splutter that soon turned into a low snore assured us he was.

Twisting unsteadily on his feet, Mason turned to me then. "As I was saying," he muttered as his tongue tried to wash the blood from his bottom lip. "You're mine."

* * *

The stack of physics textbooks looked well worn, flipped through a thousand times. I assumed Mason had bought them secondhand from another student. Perhaps he came from a poor family. Perhaps he'd gotten those muscles as a teenager working at the local gas station during summer vacation in some tiny Midwest town, topless as he pumped gas into old Chevys, his manly hair only just beginning to sprout across his chest as it grew broader by the day. Or perhaps he worked weekends on a building site, lugging bricks to pay his way through college, his large hands lifting, stacking, pulling, jacking. The fact was, I knew nothing about him, had never set eyes on this beautiful buff creature before.

And yet he knew my name.

"Are you comfortable, Ethan?" He seemed nervous now that it was just the two of us. He had washed the blood from his face. Bruises were already forming.

"How did you know my name?" I was sitting uncomfortably on the edge of the bed in his small room, like a nervous child in the house of a strange spider-haired aunt. Only Mason was no spider-haired aunt. Here in his domain, with his bruises and his cuts, he seemed sexier than ever. Yet there I was, meek and utterly intimidated, rubbing my wrists, which had become chafed and swollen from the ropes. I was no longer naked, at least not quite. Mason had generously put a towel around me. He himself was still dressed only in his gym shorts, which seemed to bulge more than ever now that we were alone.

"You're hurt," he said, noticing me rubbing my wrists. He successfully avoided my question by sitting on the bed beside me. "May I?" His voice was soft and caring as he took my forearm tenderly in his hands. His own knuckles were red and grazed, yet all his concern was focused on my wrist. He placed my forearm in his lap and I could distinctly feel his dick hardening against my skin. He began massaging my wrist, pressing it slightly into his groin.

I gulped and felt my guard shoot up—where was my woolen vest, my glasses, a book to put my head in? "We should study." I glanced at the red digits of his old clock radio on the bedside table. It was almost two in the morning. "We're running out of time. I'm supposed to help you study, remember? You didn't get the living hell beaten out of you for no reason."

"No, I didn't," he said, and I felt his cock swell even more against my forearm.

I tried to get up, although I didn't really want to. It was just a polite gesture, a nervous reaction. I pretended to make for the pile of textbooks, but Mason easily pulled me back on the bed.

"You liked watching me fight," he remarked. He was looking at the pole beneath my towel extending higher and higher. "It turned you on?" he asked, as if not wanting to make the assumption. Humility in the handsome is a rare treat and the ultimate turn-on in my opinion. My shaft shot to its full height beneath the towel.

I managed to conceal the tremor in my voice. "Yes."

Mason began to blush. "I like watching you, too."

I was confused. "What do you mean?"

"I've seen you around campus. You're so...cute. You probably never noticed, but I sit behind you in lectures. One row back and three to the left. Sometimes I follow you after class, at least until you get to the turnoff to your dorm. You've always got your head in a book, even when you're walking, do you know that?"

I nodded, not sure what to say. I was embarrassed, more nervous than ever. Nobody had ever admitted to watching me before. I didn't think anyone had a reason to. "Why would *you* watch *me*?"

Mason shrugged coyly. "I don't know. Because you're not like the other guys I hang around with. You're not like me."

"Opposites attract." The words came out of my mouth before I even realized it.

Mason smiled and I could see his heart skip a beat beneath his massive, trimmed chest. "Is that another one of the laws of physics?"

"No, that's one of the laws of love." *Ouch!* I grimaced at my painfully corny one-liner, but Mason just smiled at me adoringly for having said it. Suddenly I suspected somewhere beneath Mason's hunky, fist-hurling façade was a fan-flapping, eyelid-fluttering, heart-swooning Jane Austen fan.

He was looking into my eyes now, occasionally glancing down just to watch my lips move. "I wish we could sit an exam for those laws." His face was closer now, moving closer still.

"It's supposed to be the other way around." I was whispering now, he was so near to me. "You seem so popular and...and perfect. I'm supposed to be the one watching you. You're not supposed to know I even exist. Are you just doing this to pass the exam?"

Mason shook his head.

"I don't get it," I breathed. "Science is the pursuit of knowledge through experimentation and reason. I need a reason for this. Why do you like me?"

"I can't give you one. Not everything is science."

With that he placed his sore, swollen lips on mine and gently kissed me.

Instantly I wanted more. My tongue parted his lips, opening the passage for both our tongues to explore each other's mouths. He took my jaw in one hand and unwrapped my towel as best he could with the other. I instinctively went for his tightly packed gym shorts, rubbing at the bulge trapped inside. He gasped through our kiss and pulled his mouth away from mine to say, "I've wanted this for so long."

Suddenly I found my courage. I grabbed the back of his head, keeping my adoring alpha male close and said, "Shut up. You sound like a line from my little sister's diary. Just shut up and fuck me."

Suddenly Mason's bruised and battered body rose off the bed, large and looming, and he seized me around the waist. He pulled me to my feet and my erection stabbed him in the stomach. He stole a kiss, then spun me about and dropped to his knees behind me.

I felt instantly vulnerable, blind, unable to see what was happening, uncertain of what I was doing here and yet somehow...safe.

The next thing I felt were his hands parting the round cheeks of my ass to make way for his hot, moist tongue.

My eyelids fluttered, I couldn't stop them.

Air slithered from my lungs and I didn't want it to return. I held my breath as that tongue slid up and down my sweaty, hungry crack, pushing against the ring of my anus, flickering inside me briefly, tauntingly, before pulling out again.

I heard him stand.

I gave a long overdue inhale and began breathing again, my head light and spinning.

Mason's hands slid away from my asscheeks and gripped me by my hips then swiveled me around to face him. He pressed his lips against mine, pushed his tongue inside my mouth and I could taste the sweet yearning of my own ass. My cock was pressed against his hard stomach, and the bulge inside his gym shorts was nudging my balls. I could sense he was in pain, aching to be set free yet waiting for me to have the pleasure of unlocking that cage.

Desire overcame my fears, and I was the one to drop to my knees this time.

My happily quivering fingers hooked the elastic waist of his gym shorts and pulled them down, gradually.

It was like unraveling a treasure map, following the hirsute trail to a beautifully manicured island of dark pubic hair. I could smell the sweet scent of his manly sweat mingling with the aroma of cum, near and inevitable. The plump stem of his shaft appeared, and suddenly my desire to see this cub in all his glory was simply too much to bear.

I stripped the gym shorts down the length of his strapping, hairy thighs and his dick flung itself through the air, missing my face by an inch to slap against his trimmed abs.

If Mason was my muscleman, then this was truly his muscle-*cock*.

It was massive, thick and sculpted, bursting with veins and heaving with confidence.

It moved up and down in front of my face, as though waiting for my lips to give it guidance, to hold it still and take it in my mouth. I opened my lips, my tongue reaching out, desperate to taste its sweetness. But before I could satiate myself, Mason took my head in his large hands and pulled me to my feet once more.

The bed was behind me and I could feel him backing me ever closer to it. I decided to taunt him in return; I didn't want to give him that much control, at least not yet. As he tried to maneuver me backward I quickly twisted the two of us around, taking Mason by sweet surprise and forcing him onto the bed.

Mason landed flat on his back on the mattress and courageously I tried to straddle him.

That's when he turned the tables once more, rolling quickly onto his side, flipping me onto the mattress. Side by side we continued kissing, elbows and knees and cocks digging into the bed and each other.

In a willing tussle he turned me flat on my back. My stiff cock smacked flat against my stomach and Mason smiled and licked his lips. I took his jaw gently in my hand and kissed his chin. At the same time, he took hold of my cock, low at the shaft, then pulled away from my lips and moved down my body. He crouched over me and pointed my pulsating dick toward his wet open mouth. Then, without another moment's hesitation, he devoured me whole.

His mouth was wide and hot, the most slippery, sublime haven my cock had ever known. His tongue navigated me around inside him, manipulating me, teasing me, sucking and releasing.

I took his bountiful black locks in both hands to steer the thrust and lunge of his hungry quest. I heard myself moan and in a reflex move Mason picked up the pace, his head bobbing faster and faster up and down my cock.

I could feel the tension welling inside me. The muscles in my hips and buttocks trembled—partly from lack of use, partly from anticipation—as they rose up to meet Mason's plunging lips. He knew as well as I did that at this pace, I wasn't going to last long.

My balls began to surge up into my body, but Mason denied them their retreat, grabbing them and pulling them down hard.

A bolt of pain, of sheer ecstasy, rocked my body. I cried out and lurched forward, my balls caught in Mason's fist, my cock still ramming in and out of his mouth.

Suddenly the muscles in my back clenched tight and arched and with Mason's head held firmly in my hands the fire, the rush, the explosion filled his mouth, my hot currents coursing into the warm wet tunnel of his throat, swirling around the head of my cock, turning his mouth into a well of cum.

Mason swallowed hard and fast, gulping down one, two, three spasmodic jets of my sweet cum.

I panted and groaned as Mason released my cock from his mouth before he choked. I watched my dick exit his mouth glistening with saliva and cum, even stiffer and thicker and bigger than when it went in. I watched Mason's mouth gasping for air, my cum overflowing from his lips and oozing onto his strong, stubble-shaded chin.

There I lay panting and moaning and spent for a moment longer until Mason stopped my groans by shoving his thumb and index finger into my mouth. I sucked on them like a starving child ravaging a nipple, unrestrained and impossible to satisfy. I sucked ravenously, as though drawing new energy from them. Then Mason pulled his mauled fingers from my mouth and replaced them with his tongue.

We lay together, him on top of me, his rigid, furry stomach pressed against mine. His bulging, bulbous cock nudged against my drained balls and he thrust it sharply into my tender sac— perhaps a little too sharply—for I flinched hard. In a reflex response I shoved my hefty hunk right off the top of me and over the edge of the bed.

Mason rolled and hit the floor beside the bed with a loud thud...before laughing hysterically, achingly.

I leaned over quickly and looked down, embarrassed and concerned. All I could think to say was, "Fuck! Sorry!"

Mason wheezed and chuckled. "I guess that's the law of gravity."

"What goes up must come down," I said, shrugging.

"Not yet it doesn't." Mason reached up, grabbed hold of my forearm and yanked me down on the floor with him.

I landed on top of him awkwardly, forcing a pained grunt

and more laughter out of him. We kissed again, more fiercely than before, our playful antics now turning passionately rough.

Without taking his lips off mine, Mason's hand felt its way up to the bedside table, opened the drawer, rummaged inside and pulled out a condom. Only then did he tear his mouth away from mine so he could bite open the wrapper, but before he could do anything with it I took the condom from him, then bravely ran my tongue all the way down his body. My lips were tickled by the hair on his chest, then his stomach. When my tongue reached the stem of his throbbing cock, I took the condom and slid it onto Mason's shaft with my fist.

Mason had already found the lube in the drawer and was passing it to me.

I squeezed a glob into my palm.

Lying flat on his back, Mason simply watched from the floor, his large stiff penis growing even harder at the sight of me massaging it with a lubed fist.

I squeezed more lubricant onto the tips of my fingers then circled the rim of my anus, gliding my index finger deep inside myself to wet my passage, relaxing the muscles. It felt good, but I was ready for something better—and bigger.

I took Mason's cock in my hand and straddled him, positioning myself over his shaft before nuzzling the head against my crack. The bulbous head pushed my asscheeks apart, eager to make its entry. It gave rise to my own cock, now suddenly rejuvenated and once more seeking attention. It grew in length and girth quickly, hardening fast and enthusiastically slapping against my stomach once more, sprinkling a few dewdrops of precum against my tensed stomach muscles...or were they leftover beads from the last orgasm? It was hard to tell. All I knew was, Mason could wait no longer. He moaned impatiently.

Taking a deep breath, I sank myself down onto his cock.

Mason rolled his head back against the floorboards, eyes shut, mouth open wide to let a loud groan of absolute pleasure escape.

At the same time I began to slide up and down his pole, slowly at first, the muscles of my warm wet ass gradually loosening, enjoying themselves, sweeping up and down with the motion of fucking, like seaweed moving with the ebb and flow of the tide.

But I wanted the tide to move faster.

I began sliding up and down Mason's cock harder, heavier. No, not sliding; grinding.

Mason began to reciprocate, thrusting his pelvis up off the floor as I came down to meet him, then pulling back as I lifted away. The movement transformed us into a well-lubed machine.

The air from my lungs came accompanied with a noise now— a soft, low moan with each breath. "Ahhh…ohhh…ahhh…"

My stiff, bobbing cock seemed to be floating free, out on its own, unattended. Occasionally it snapped upward and smacked my stomach. Other times it bounced so hard with the rhythm that it slapped against Mason's fur-lined abs, making muffled drum-beats. Mason reined it in by seizing the shaft in one hand. He began stroking it. His palm was dry but my meat was still moist with his saliva. As the pace of penetration grew more and more intense, his fist squeezed harder and pounded my cock faster.

My groans grew louder.

"Ahhh…I…I'm…cu…"

Mason pushed himself deeper and faster into me.

I rode him harder. Harder still.

He grunted, teeth clenched, as though he was back in the fight, determined to win.

I panted and groaned, words still trying to push their way out of my heaving lungs.

"I'm cu...I'm cum..."

Before I could spit it out, the head of my cock bloomed large and purple and its slit beaded up with another gleaming ball of precum, ready to do some spitting of its own.

My second orgasm in only a few minutes was even bigger and more powerful than the first. As my eyes closed and my mouth fell open and my head rolled back, I fired a blast of cum that soared over Mason's ribbed stomach and landed on the muscle of his chest, catching in the web of hair coating his meaty pecs.

As soon as the sizzling jism made contact, Mason's balls opened their own floodgates. He arched his back high, pushing himself as far into me as he could. Still groaning and rocking with ecstasy, I pressed my asscheeks down hard against his pelvis, eating up the entire length of his cock.

I felt Mason's head high inside me.

I felt the temperature skyrocket as the head of his condom bulged with an immense load of boiling hot cum.

Mason's body jolted once, twice, and again and again, each time shooting another pulse of cum from his shaft.

It triggered a second load of cum from my own cock, this time with less trajectory and more spent pain, the white spool landing in a shining loop across Mason's tight, hairy belly.

I gasped then, spasming with more sharp pain as Mason tried to gently, slowly, massage the last of the juice from my swollen cock. Gradually he lowered his hips to the floor as the last of his own cum spilled into the condom inside me.

For a moment we both stayed that way, speechless and exhausted. Then Mason sat up, his cock still in me, and wrapped his beefy arms around my torso. My tender shaft was pressed between our stomachs, the smooth skin of my heaving belly and chest prickled by his muscular, manicured torso. My cum smeared us both.

He kissed me then, a long, deep, passionate kiss. And when it was done, I looked into his eyes and whispered, "So much for studying. I'm sorry, but I think you're going to fail that physics exam."

Mason simply smiled. Like someone who knew better.

I failed the physics exam.

I spent so much time enjoying my hard-on and glancing across the examination hall at Mason that my distractions resulted in my first-ever F. I was proud of it. After all, Mason was right— not everything is science. And science isn't everything.

I wore my failed grade like a badge of honor, for it came with memories of the best fuck of my life.

Mason passed the exam with flying colors.

At first I was completely bewildered. I thought he must have cheated, or been extremely lucky, or perhaps even slept with our professor. But as I got to know him—sitting *next to each other* in lectures, walking back to my dorm *together* after class, spending nights studying and kissing and fucking and waking up in each other's arms—I realized Mason was not a cheat. He didn't rely on luck, nor did he sleep with anyone to make the grade. Mason was in fact a straight-A student and had been all along.

That night in the attic, he didn't need to win me to pass the exam.

He didn't *need* me at all.

He simply wanted me, right from the beginning.

Just as I wanted him, his muscle *and* his mind, in the end.

My end.

BOBBY LO VERSUS THE EVIL SAKATA

Thomas Fuchs

Bobby Lo studied himself in his full-length mirror and was deeply satisfied. He flexed an arm and smiled as his biceps bulged like a fist trying to punch its way through the flesh of his arm. He raised both arms over his head, accentuating the carved ridges of his torso. Excellent definition. And he had to admit that he was hung pretty nice, too. His dick was thick and heavy, nestled in its glossy black bush, a powerful snake lying in wait. His legs were as solid as tree trunks.

He was turning himself on. His dick curled upward toward his abs. Precum oozed. He let his head roll back, thought of gorgeous guys he had fucked and then, after several minutes of delicious sensation, at the moment of release, snapped his head forward, opened his eyes and shot—load after load of heavy, rich cum splattering onto the glass. He was the picture of strength, a bottomless lake of energy. He glistened with it. He had no idea that it was this very aura of power that would soon attract the attention of a mysterious and very dangerous old man.

Bobby wasn't just a muscle boy with a show-off bod. Although he hadn't competed for some time and only gave lessons when he needed to make a little extra money, he was known and well respected in the world of martial arts. A good friend of his, Harold Smith, was the sensei of a highly regarded dojo with a very select membership. So it was no great surprise to Bobby that he had been invited to attend when Smith hosted the venerable Sakata-san, an ancient master visiting from Japan.

Actually, Bobby had only heard vaguely of Sakata, some odd bits here and there. The old man was said to have dropped a charging bull with a glancing blow. Someone said he had been a special teacher for Imperial troops during World War II, but for that to be true he would have to be very old, indeed. Maybe his reputation and that of some earlier master had gotten mixed up in the storytelling. One account had him giving a demonstration for Admiral Perry, back when the Americans first came to Japan. But of course that was in 1854 and was therefore impossible. What most interested Bobby was that Sakata was said to possess very ancient, deadly knowledge which had never been written down and had been passed on only by personal instruction from one generation to another for centuries, perhaps millennia.

As Bobby cleaned himself up after his session of self-admiration, he considered what he should wear to Sakata's demonstration that afternoon. It had to be something casual enough that he could participate in the demonstration if he got a chance but not so casual as to seem disrespectful. These old Japanese masters could be so damn demanding and were sometimes a little peculiar in their demands. Hard to read. Inscrutable, actually. He laughed as the cliché passed through his head.

He pulled on a nice T-shirt, not a muscle shirt, and sweats that were baggy but still tight enough across the seat to show off his legs and his fine ass. *Never hurts to look good* was one of Bobby's mottos.

He drove south down the Hollywood Freeway, to Little Tokyo, and then across the tracks into the old warehouse district, where his friend Smith leased the building he had turned into his dojo. When Bobby got there, Smith was greeting his guests as they stepped up onto the loading dock, which had been converted into a porch shaded by bamboo and decorated with flowering plants. It was lovely and only highlighted something Bobby noticed immediately. He hadn't seen Smith for a while and he was struck by the fact that his friend looked tired and pale, as though he wasn't sleeping well or was recovering from the flu. Drained.

When he asked Smith if he was okay, Smith smiled and said he was fine and to just go on in. A dozen or so other guests had already arrived. Bobby recognized most of them, drawn from the cream of Smith's classes. There were greetings, some social chitchat. A few minutes passed, a few more guests arrived and then Smith came in, closing the door behind him and going to the center of the large workout mat that was the chief feature of the room.

As everyone seated himself around the perimeter of the mat, conversation ceased and expectations rose. And then, so gracefully that he almost seemed to glide, Sakata appeared from a small side room, joining Smith on the mat.

Bobby was impressed. Sakata was old all right, maybe in his seventies, as dark and hard as carved teak, but when he smiled and bowed in greeting, he seemed to radiate strength and friendly warmth. Smith made a few introductory remarks and then Sakata spoke, in English with little accent. Surprising. How many skills did this old master posses?

Sakata explained that the real secret to his attack technique lay in striking in ways his opponent would never expect.

Explanation was about to become demonstration. The master quickly scanned the guests, looked at Bobby for a second... but then, to Bobby's disappointment, passed on and gestured to another man, a hulking 250-pound Polynesian known to everyone simply as "Tut."

As Tut got to the center of the mat, Sakata asked him to take his fighting stance, then pointed out that Tut had his arms up and slightly forward, a pose common to almost all fighters, whatever their style. "Now watch," said Sakata, and made a quick feint toward Tut, who automatically blocked with his arms at the same time that he moved his body out of the way of Sakata's strike.

"You see," said the old master, "he assumes I'm trying to hit his body or his head, but my target really is..." and quick as a flash he reached out and gave a sharp tap to points on the lower parts of one of Tut's arms. The big man collapsed to the mat as though a great weight had been dropped on him.

Sakata did a quick revival technique on the fallen man, rubbing the back of his neck and shoulders. When Tut was able to get back on his feet, Sakata spent some time explaining just what points he had hit and what the correct striking techniques were for each. Then he sent the big Polynesian back to his seat and said, "Of course, there are other routes for surprise attack." This time, he nodded to Bobby to come on to the mat.

"Ready to fight?" asked the old man.

"Always, Sensei," Bobby replied.

Sakata smiled approvingly, bowed and attacked. As Bobby expected, the old man darted in as though to strike at his arms and he was ready to dodge this. But Bobby's arms were not the target. Instead, moving so quickly that he was almost a blur, the old man swept behind Bobby and hit a spot he hadn't shown the class—just below the base of Bobby's spine, at the very edge of his asscrack.

Bobby's legs buckled, opening the crack nice and wide so that Sakata could make his second strike—a point right on the rim of Bobby's asshole—and the instant he did, a stunning shock like lightning sweep through Bobby, leaving him completely helpless and unable to protect himself from Sakata's deadly finishing move. The old master wrapped his arms around Bobby's torso, torquing his spine from the base of his neck to the small of his back, which he could have easily snapped. He didn't, of course; this was only a demonstration. But before he let go, he gave Bobby a compliment, whispering in his ear, "You did well. At least you stayed on your feet." Then he blew into Bobby's ear. His breath was strangely warm and stimulating.

Bobby steadied himself, the strength slowly coming back into him. Then he realized there was one problem—his dick was ramrod stiff. It was a good thing his sweats *were* baggy. Maybe Master Sakata wouldn't notice. But the old man smiled and gave his dick a solid whack with his palm, at about midpoint, and down it went. Bobby turned red as he made his way back to the edge of the mat. No one said anything about it. These things happened sometimes.

Later, as everyone was leaving and saying good-bye to the master, Sakata looked Bobby in the eye and gave him an order, "I will see you again. Tonight, here. Ten o'clock."

Although Bobby usually resisted any kind of order, he found himself bowing and saying, "Yes. Thank you." He was intensely curious about what the old man had in store for him. What secret teaching would be revealed?

Because this was a warehouse district, there were few streetlights. When Bobby returned that night, the streets were dark, deserted and silent. Just as he stepped onto the porch, the door flew open and Smith appeared. "Go on in," he said, quickly, nervously. "He's waiting for you." He continued to his car, got in and disappeared into the night. Bobby wondered what was going on.

The lights were off in the warehouse, the only illumination coming from a few flickering candles. A faint scent of incense tinted the air. Bobby didn't know what it was, but he thought it smelled a lot like cum. This was beginning to look like it wasn't going to be about martial arts.

"Good evening," said Sakata, stepping out of the shadows. He offered a thin smile but no bow, none of the usual courtesies. He had changed from the judo outfit he had been wearing earlier to a silk kimono, wrapped tightly, as though he was cold.

"Is everything all right?" asked Bobby. "Should I come some other time? Tomorrow?"

"No!" said Sakata, suddenly animated by urgency. He led Bobby to the mat. A thick silk carpet now lay in the middle of it, marked with Chinese characters that Bobby recognized as very old and abstract signs for earth, air, water and fire—the four elements, the pillars of the Universe.

Sakata seemed concerned with positioning himself and Bobby at the very center of the carpet. That done, he put a hand on one of Bobby's biceps, like a connoisseur appraising a fine statue. "Ah," he said quietly, "such strength."

Bobby didn't usually go for old men, but Sakata was in shape and probably had a fine sexual technique. Maybe he could learn something from him in that department as well as about martial arts.

"The young have so much energy," said Sakata, moving his hand to Bobby's powerful chest. His touch was gentle but there was nothing tentative about it. He was a master, after all. Rhythmically, he alternated sweeping passes along Bobby's chest with a vibrating finger-squeeze of his nipples. With his other hand, he stroked Bobby's abs, and then brought both hands to the area just below Bobby's navel, where he did a slow, deep, circulating massage.

Bobby's dick strained hard against his sweats but still Sakata didn't touch him there. The old man lifted his hands from Bobby and told him to take off his shirt. Bobby did and, without being asked, also dropped his sweats. He stood naked and hard before the great Sakata, who dropped suddenly to his knees.

With the tip of his tongue, Sakata began working magic on the tip of Bobby's dick, creating a kind of dancing tingling so stimulating that despite himself, Bobby, whose control was superb and who wanted nothing more than to prolong this exquisite sensation, soon felt precum seeping from him.

The old man moved on, taking in all of Bobby's thick, throbbing cock, closing his mouth over him, capturing him completely. Then, the rhythmic wet sliding sucking began. Bobby really was being worked over by a master.

Soon Bobby was shaking and groaning with ecstasy and soon after that, Sakata went for his finishing move, suddenly striking with an iron finger at the same point he had used on Bobby in combat that afternoon, right at the edge of his hole, a blow which again sent lightning flashing through Bobby and this time made him shoot a full, hot load down the willing throat of the old man. Then the master struck again and Bobby shot, and again, and again.

When Bobby finally had nothing left for him, Sakata sat back on his haunches and smiled. A thick string of Bobby's cum dribbled from the side of his mouth. He caught it with a finger, licked it up, and smiled again. Then he closed his eyes and seemed to fold in upon himself in some intense form of meditation. His lips were moving slightly but there was no sound. Instead, Bobby

could feel a low vibration emanating from the man. Then to
Bobby's growing astonishment, his features softened, his skin
getting smoother until it was free of the lines and crevices of age,
until he seemed a much younger version of the old man who had
just been there, almost boyish.

Bobby stepped forward for a closer look at this extraordi-
nary transformation, but as he did so, he was suddenly dizzy,
completely exhausted—drained. He sat down, then lay back on
the mat. He would rest. For just a moment. So he thought.

When he woke, Sakata was gone. The candles had burned
out; there was a soft light coming from somewhere outside. It
was dawn. He had been asleep for hours but when he got to his
feet he felt heavy and tired.

Late that afternoon, he was napping at home when Smith
woke him with his call. "How you doing?" he asked as soon as
Bobby said hello.

"A little knocked out, to tell you the truth. It was a long
night. A little strange."

"I know."

"Yeah, I'll bet you do," said Bobby.

"We have to talk," said Smith. "I'm coming over."

When Smith arrived he told Bobby a lot about Sakata, much
of which Bobby had already begun to suspect. Old as the old
man appeared to be, Smith believed him to in fact be a great
deal older. Of all the many secret techniques he had mastered
over the—well, maybe it was centuries—there were ones that
enable a man to prolong his vitality forever. Sakata was a kind
of vampire, but it wasn't blood that he needed.

"You know," said Bobby, "there's a lot of bull crap that goes
around about Asian secrets. A lot of stuff just to frighten people
and all that, but not true."

"Yeah," said Smith, "but you know a lot of it is true. We've both seen some strange stuff. And think about what happened to you last night. And look what he's been doing to me."

"You do look a little fucked up," said Bobby. "Sick, sort of."

Smith nodded wearily. "Not to give blow jobs a bad name, but he's sucking me dry. I'll admit it was pretty hot at first, but now he's killing me."

Suddenly Bobby was angry. "Did you know all this when you invited me and the others? You must have."

Smith admitted he had.

"I'm not sure how I feel about you setting me up," said Bobby.

"Would you have believed me if you hadn't gone through all that last night?" asked Smith.

Bobby had to admit that his friend had a point, and then he asked, "How did you find out about him? Did you know when he came here? How did he wind up at your place, anyway?"

Smith explained that Sakata had contacted him via email from a small dojo in Osaka, flattering him with talk about how Smith was famous, known even in Japan. When the master said that he would be visiting Los Angeles, Smith was quick to offer his hospitality.

"The first night he was here I began to get the picture," said Smith. "Now I'm stuck with him. He doesn't seem to have any plans for going back. I think maybe something went wrong for him in Japan and he has to stay away for a while. I don't know how to get rid of him."

Bobby respected Smith and liked him. They had tricked a few times and then moved on to a fine friendship, and he was always willing to help a friend, but what was he supposed to do?

"To tell you the truth," said Smith, "I think he's shopping. Looking for someone to replace me."

"Well, so there's no problem," said Bobby. "He'll just move on to someone else."

"No, you see, he really likes the dojo. Wants to use it to recruit new guys to suck. That's what yesterday's demonstration was really about. He wants to take the place over completely. Without me. That's what I'm thinking."

"Now, how is he going to do that?"

"I don't like the way he's been looking at me the past few days," said Smith.

"Are you serious? You don't really think...?"

Smith nodded. "He could do it in an instant, and make it look like a heart attack or a stroke or something."

Bobby had to admit that was true. This was serious. They talked further and Bobby finally promised that he would try to come up with a plan for getting rid of Sakata. "It's got to be pretty good," said Bobby "Sakata's no one to fool around with. If we're gonna get him, we gotta get him good."

"Okay, but soon, okay?" said Smith.

Bobby suggested that in the meantime Smith should drink a lot of ginseng. "Get the kind that restores your semen," he advised. Then, just as his friend was leaving, Bobby, being Bobby, asked a question he couldn't resist. "Did the old guy say anything about last night?"

"Oh, yes," said Smith. "It seems you gave him plenty of what he needs. He was quite disappointed when I told him you weren't a student of mine."

Bobby nodded. He was pleased but not surprised.

Immediately after Smith left, Bobby Googled for information about how cum eating might prolong vitality. He didn't find much. There was a long entry on Wikipedia but he wasn't sure it was reliable. He turned to his collection of old books, and was soon deep in tales about flesh-eating goblins and spirit thieves.

There were only a few allusions to men who did what Sakata seemed to be doing.

Days passed. Smith called a number of times, once half-seriously suggesting they ought to just kill the old man. "Out of the question," said Bobby. "For one thing, I'm not sure how to do it. Some of the stuff I've read suggests he may have the power to ward off bullets and knives. Also, suppose we're wrong. We're not, I'm sure, but if we are...well, killing someone is kind of a mistake you can't fix."

"Okay," said Smith, "but you'd better come up with something. One of these days I'm not going to be able to cum anymore and that could be the end for me. Besides, he's giving some classes and he's managed to recruit some guys from them so he's pretty well set up to get what he needs to keep going."

"Has he asked about me?" said Bobby.

"A few times but not for a while now."

"Huh," said Bobby, not at all sure how he felt about that.

Finally, Bobby did the one thing he hadn't done for a while, the thing that was really the most difficult for him. He sat quietly and did some meditation, some thinking. Stillness, an emptiness into which something might come.

The old technique worked. He remembered something he had read once, maybe years ago. It was in a book he had but hadn't bothered to check, since it wasn't about witchcraft and monsters. It was a collection of very romantic stories about what the old Japanese sometimes called "comrade love." There was a reference in it, something he had barely noticed, only half remembered—yes, there it was. The passage described evil men who prolonged their lives for centuries by draining the cum from strong young men. It also said these evil ones could themselves be rendered helpless—at least temporarily—by having the cum drained from them. Now Bobby knew what he had to do. Surely

Sakata would resist but if anyone could make this plan work, it was Bobby Lo.

He needed to get a few things done. First, he went to the hardware store and bought some yards of clothesline. The clerk who helped him was a cute boy who flirted with a few teasing questions about what Bobby was planning to do with the cord. Bobby was friendly and made a mental note to come back soon and see if this guy was really interested in learning about hojo-jitsu, the Japanese art of tying people up. Bobby had spent a long time practicing this and he had gotten very good at it.

Next, he went to a shipping company, where he got information on overseas delivery, and bought a nice, solid, wooden crate.

He had pretty much recovered from his session with Sakata, but before dealing with the strange old master again, he had to be in the best possible condition. Lots of cardio, alternated with his systematic weight program. After a series of intense sessions, when he felt he was at his peak, mouth-watering and brimming with energy, he got Smith to come over again and explained his plan. "Tell Sakata I want to see him again."

Smith was a little doubtful about Bobby's plan but Bobby was confident.

"You always are," said Smith, "but if this doesn't work…"

"I don't like to let things drag on," said Bobby as he gave Smith the rope. "Let's do this now. Just don't lose your nerve, okay?"

Later, Smith called from the dojo. Sakata was delighted that Bobby wanted to return. He was expecting him that very evening.

"I'll be there," said Bobby. "You better be, too."

As Bobby approached the dojo this time, he was struck by the sense of dreariness that seemed to hang over the building. It had been little more than a week since he'd been there last and the weather hadn't been particularly hot, but the bamboo plants on the porch looked withered and the blossoming plants were shriveling.

When Sakata let Bobby in, he didn't see Smith, and could only hope he was close by, hadn't panicked and fled or, was it possible?, had already been disposed of by Sakata.

"It's so good to see you again," said Sakata, as he led Bobby to the rug marked with mystic symbols.

"Thank you, Master. It is my honor."

"Why have you come?" asked Sakata. "Some of the boys have been reluctant to return after their session with me." Was the old man suspicious, had he any inkling of what Bobby had planned for him?

A perfect answer, combining flattery with self-interest, popped into Bobby's head: "Master, I hope to learn from you."

Sakata seemed satisfied. He asked Bobby to take off his shirt.

Bobby did so and then, at a nod from Sakata dropped his sweats. Sakata studied him, smiled, said again, "Your energy is very strong. I think even stronger than before."

"I prepared myself for you."

Sakata skipped the nipple play this time, going right to Bobby's cock, the effect of his silken touch so immediate and powerful that Bobby had trouble speaking for a moment. Then he said, "Master, I have a special request."

"What?" asked Sakata, irritated at being interrupted. Having gotten Bobby hard he was about to begin sucking. "What do you want?"

Master," Bobby tried again, "It is impertinent of me to ask, but...I want to experience your force. Master, I want you to fuck me. Please."

The old man was so startled by the request, he let go of Bobby, who immediately dropped to all fours and assumed the position many lucky men had found irresistible in the past, with his chest lowered to the ground and his magnificent ass riding high.

"Please, Master," he said. He kept his head lowered in obsequiousness, but out of the corner of his eye he saw the old man's rod tenting his flowered kimono.

Still Sakata did nothing so Bobby turned, got hold of the old man's cock—it was half erect—and stroked it with the technique called "searching butterfly," a fine fluttering touch on the tip. The old man's dick grew and stiffened to iron. It went no higher than just straight out, but that was pretty good for an old man, and more than enough to do the job. The only question was, would Sakata be able to resist giving Bobby what Bobby needed to get from him?

Bobby fingered the area just under the old man's balls and was pleased to feel some pressure in the tube leading from the prostate, semen being summoned up, making its way through... but when he checked the base of his cock and felt the tightened ligaments he realized Sakata was using a "hold-back" technique, blocking the flow. Of course, this would allow him to have an orgasm, quite a powerful one in fact, without actually losing any of his precious cum. That wouldn't do at all. Bobby wasn't going to allow this old monster to fuck him without being drained to the deep. He went back to using the butterfly touch and then quickly replaced his fingers with his tongue, warm and wet and just as agile as his fingers,

Sakata's self-control slipped. Bobby tasted precum. Yes! He whipped back around into the "Please fuck me" position, ass in the air...and the old man, unable to resist this delicious temptation, began pushing into him.

Bobby's muscle control was superb, squeezing Sakata from the tip on down, then relaxing, letting the old man push in farther, then squeezing, over and over until the old man was deep inside Bobby, gasping and grunting and pounding away. This went on for some time and then the pumping stopped and the old man was shaking and shivering and Bobby thought, "This is it! He's going to shoot!" but damn it, Sakata was using the hold-back technique, prolonging his ecstasy and, most critically, holding on to his semen, his vital force. Soon he would pull out and have his mouth at Bobby's dick, sucking up more of Bobby's essence.

Bobby squeezed Sakata's dick with his butt muscles, harder than before, determined to keep him trapped until he got what he wanted. The old man tapped Bobby's back, the classic martial arts signal of submission, meaning, "let go." Bobby responded by bucking and grinding his hips. The old man tried to escape but Bobby held him and worked him.

Finally the old man groaned in despair and shot a great hot load and still Bobby held on to him, making him shoot twice more until, still held tightly, Sakata collapsed onto Bobby's back. Bobby released him and he rolled onto the mat, completely exhausted, in a kind of stupor.

Bobby called out for Smith, but he needn't have bothered because his friend had been watching the whole thing from the shadows and now rushed forward with the rope.

Sakata was too weak to resist Bobby's quick, efficient work and soon the master was trussed up like a chicken ready for roasting, with his arms behind him and bound tightly to his ankles. Bobby finished the job by tying a gag tightly in place. The old man wouldn't be able to make a sound.

After that, it was easy for Bobby and Smith to get Sakata into the box. The old man seemed to revive slightly and the last Bobby saw of him as he slid the lid into place were the old man's eyes looking up at him, blazing with fury. It was, Bobby had to admit to himself, a little frightening, but it stilled any doubts he may have harbored or any tendency toward mercy. The old man was dangerous and had to go back to where he had come from.

Bobby and Smith went directly to the shipping office with their cargo. It cost a lot to send Sakata back to Osaka but Smith was happy to pay.

Later, Smith told Bobby that he thought maybe he should give up the lease on the dojo and move to another town in case Sakata ever came back looking for revenge. Bobby said there was no point in that because both of them were well-enough known that Sakata could always track them down wherever they went. If he did ever turn up again, they'd just handle him again. Bobby really didn't want to think about it. His mind was on that cute clerk in the hardware store. He had to go back there soon and see what he could make happen.

A few weeks later, Smith received a puzzled letter from the Osaka dojo. The box had been delivered but it was empty. There was a hole about three-by-three feet on one side, as though something had gnawed its way out.

DETAILS

Natty Soltesz

People don't get it. They turn their heads, their jaws drop in
awe, but they don't appreciate the time it takes for him to
look so good, the work that goes into such beauty.

Which maybe explains why he went home with me that night;
why he didn't shrink from my gaze when I spotted him across
the club. He saw in my eyes that I understood his dedication.
That I was *grateful* for it.

It took him over an hour to get ready to go out. That *didn't*
include styling his hair, or washing his clothes, or last-minute
push-ups or a dozen other necessary, invisible rituals.

Also, obviously, there was the gym: two hours a day, six days
a week, religiously, devotionally. It wasn't a question of when or
if (and it was his contention that if you were the type to say, "I
have to go to the gym," you were clearly doomed and probably
wasting not just your money but the resource of the gym itself).
It wasn't a question. He lived to work out. There were times in
the early evening darkness when he would get out of his car and

see the gym before him, its inner light creating a glow around the place, and he would feel something like awe for what it was and what it meant to him.

He knew how to work his body so that it didn't *look like* he used the gym, by which I mean he didn't appear over-worked or out of proportion—no bulging breasts or chicken legs. He looked like a man: wide, rocky back; flared chest; solid arms; baseball biceps; tight, nubby stomach; firm, round ass; tree-trunk thighs; cut calves. He researched this stuff: he had seven subscriptions to various men's health and style and muscle magazines (some more reputable than others).

Of course, good genes didn't hurt. He'd had a nice body in high school even before he'd begun working out. People would say, "There goes another one of those gorgeous Abrito boys," but he turned out to be the most gorgeous of all.

He tanned, of course. In the spring and summer he was on the roof of his apartment building for a few hours during any given week. In the winter he used a tanning salon. But he knew when to stop—he spent just enough time to get a glow. He tanned nude, thinking it ridiculous to ignore any part of your body. In the beds you had to be careful to spread your legs, though, or you'd get white creases under your asscheeks.

It was just this sort of attention to detail that was lost on people. A good haircut wasn't cheap, and he had his straight brown hair cut at least once a month. Then, of course, he had to shave, especially before hitting the club. His face, obviously, but he also shaved most of the rest of his body—chest, armpits. He left a trimmed brown brush of pubes over his cock, but kept his scrotum hairless and of course he shaved his ass—the cheeks and also around his asshole.

That was never a picnic, but he'd gotten used to it. He would lie on the bathroom floor and throw his legs over his head. Using a handheld mirror for accuracy was critical. The cheeks were easy—like running a razor over twin bowling balls. The crack was more treacherous, so he was careful around the sensitive skin of his anus, making sure he got every little hair.

This had to be done at least once a week but the results were worth it. He'd even take a second, once he wiped off the shaving cream, to admire his shorn butt—the creamy curves, his pert pink pucker. He'd never actually had a girl go back there, but you never knew, and most importantly, *he'd* know.

In the shower he'd take care to wash around and in everything he could—even going so far as to poke a soapy finger up his butthole, which was tight and perfect.

Then he dried off and moisturized all over—chest, legs, cock, balls, ass.

Next came cologne. He'd heard people say that they didn't like cologne on guys, that it was overdoing it, but for him there was no question. Cologne was the one thing that brought it all together, a sort of sexual aura that hovered. It told the world, without anybody even having to see you, that you cared about yourself and what others thought. He used Dolce & Gabbana, splashed it on his neck, chest, and yeah, even down there. He'd slide some on his pelvis, both sides, then bend over and smack a cologne-infused finger against his asshole.

He didn't dress like the typical club-going douche bag, either. He liked designer stuff, not too flashy, but stylish; button-down shirts, tailored to fit, black or gray, typically; a nice pair of pants that showed off the goods; designer briefs of course—French cut, tight, with a nice big pocket in front.

All told he probably spent twenty hours a week on himself, he'd figured out once. It was practically a part-time job, but it was his greatest accomplishment.

* * *

The club was the place to show it off, the fruits of his labor. As much as he'd always gotten a thrill over the fleeting attention he received—the girls coming up to him, *oooing* and *aahing* with their girlfriends as they ran their hands over his arms and chest, pressing against the muscle; the guys complimenting his physique, grilling him about his routine—he'd become impressed with the shallowness of it all. With girls, it always eventually came back to them. And guys invariably saw him as a threat.

So I think what I saw that night, what gave me the courage to actually walk up and talk to this paradigm, this *god*, was the look of curiosity—no, reprieve—that washed over his face. Maybe he knew I was a fag. Maybe he didn't care. Or maybe he suspected that I *got it*, that I not only wanted the incomparable gift that he had to offer, but that I also knew the great heights that he'd reached with himself. After all, I was no slouch myself. But I was nowhere near this guy's level.

"Dull night," I said to him.

"When isn't it?" he said, and smiled a brilliant, meticulously whitened smile.

"It's not feeling like it is anymore," I said boldly. Uncertainty crossed his face. "Did you see me looking at you?"

"Yeah," he said. "But so is everybody else."

"With good reason," I said, and bought us both a drink. He drank his in one big gulp. "I'm sure I don't have to tell you how many calories are in that," I said.

"It's not smart to over-deny yourself," he said, and shrugged. "I'm cutting loose."

I pointed to a group of girls at the corner of the bar, looking his way, drooling in their cosmo glasses. "I'm sure they'd be happy to join you," I said.

"Yeah, but something tells me you'd rather they didn't," he

said, and I laughed. He was savvier than I'd anticipated.

"That's up to you," I said, and ordered us another round; again he promptly downed his.

"I've never done anything like this before," he said.

"What *are* you doing?"

"You tell me."

"Careful," I said, and he laughed, and we had yet another drink, but he drank his slowly this time.

"I have a Jacuzzi in my…mansion," I said, before I could stop myself.

"And you're so modest," he said.

"I try. But you know, Jacuzzis are good for the muscles. The skin too."

"Not really," he said. "But it sounds pretty relaxing anyway. I'll drive my own car and follow you, and I'm not making any promises."

"We'll hang out. I have my own gym. I have a sauna, too."

"Really?"

"Yeah, but I might be out of clean towels for you to wear."

"We'll see," he said, practically rolling his eyes, which I took as a good sign, because to humor me meant that there was respect coming from his end—respect that was mutual, and I think he grasped that, too.

I showed him around my place and had Henry fire up the Jacuzzi. My guest was impressed with the gym, I think, on which I had not scrimped. I gave him a bathing suit, but he was frisky enough to leave it off, so that when he joined me in the Jacuzzi he just whipped off his towel with a smirk and there he was. And beautiful though the whole package was, (perfectly sized, hanging nicely flaccid), it also seemed natural to me that he should be naked, like his clothes were just so much propriety.

"You can stand there for another minute if you want," I said, but he'd already begun to slide into the water. His leg slipped against mine and he let it stay there. He said he'd had way too much to drink. He said I was trying to take advantage of him, and I told him he was absolutely right.

"I don't know what I'm doing here," he said, resting his head on the back of the tub, looking up at the stars.

"You're here, I'd suspect, because the idea of me sucking your dick doesn't seem half bad. You're thinking, *He's nice enough. He's not some fat ugly thing. Why shouldn't I give him a thrill?*"

"I think you're right," he said, and despite my carefully cultivated attitude of being above it all, my heart fluttered and my stomach knotted up. He saw it in my eyes, I think, because he got really teasing. He started running his hands up and down his perfect torso, his wet chest, his stomach, raising his body upward out of the water until I could see that his prick was hard, bobbing in the bubbles.

He gave me a show. He was kind of awkward; it was like he was trying this behavior on for size, but it was undoubtedly turning him on (me too, obviously). He arched his back and stroked his prick; he turned over and lifted his ass out of the water, letting me examine every crack and crevice.

"You want to touch me?" he asked.

"Yes, please," I said, sounding like Oliver with his empty bowl. He let me run my hands over his solid arms, his perfect chest. Everything was so slick and smooth in the water. He let me touch his ridged stomach. He let me handle his balls and stroke his dick, for a minute. I wrapped my hands around his sturdy legs, rubbed them up and down. I kissed his feet. Then he turned over.

I turned to his back and let my fingers glide down the slot of his spine to his perfect asscheeks. He surprised me by resting his knees on the step and spreading his ass out for me. I think he'd been waiting to do that for somebody for a long time.

I returned his perceived gratitude by eating him out properly. I spent a long time just tonguing the perfect muscled cheeks of his ass, even biting them, which made him squirm. I did some quick swipes with my tongue along his crack, just barely tasting his hole. When I felt underneath that he was hard and ready, I jammed my tongue against his hole. I rimmed around it in circles, lapped it up hard and glided across it softly.

But I guess I was still being too tentative because when I came up for air he reached back and slipped his own finger inside himself.

"That's what you wanted to do, isn't it?"

"Oh, yeah."

"Mmmm, it feels good," he said, and he slipped another finger inside.

"I want to fuck that ass," I said.

"I bet you do," he said. "You know you're barely worthy."

"I know," I said, stroking my dick which was so, so hard. "I know but it's so hot. You're so hot."

"Everybody wants this ass," he said. "But you're the first person who's ever asked. That's the only reason I'm letting you."

That was fine with me. I grabbed a condom and my lube. As I got us both ready I knew that part of what he was saying was true, but also that he was just as turned on as I was by the thought of somebody using him. People do things all the time for their own satisfaction, but that's a lonely business, and everyone eventually needs to be appreciated for what they've got.

He was tight. I had to take my time. Fortunately he knew how to relax himself, to control his muscles to allow me in. Then I pushed it in him to the hilt, or he sat back and devoured me, either way.

I started feeling like I wanted to get my nut. I was grabbing hold of his asscheeks with each hand, fucking away, and he was grunting so I figured it was okay for him but then he took one of my hands kind of forcefully and brought it to his cock. So I started stroking him and he was so, so hard, and that was when it really started to get good. We got a rhythm going.

"You like my ass?" he said.

"Oh, my god, yes. It's so tight."

"How often do you get a piece like this? If ever?"

"No, nothing like this ever."

"Better than any girls you've ever had?"

"Better than any girls, or guys, or anything."

"That's right. Fuck me."

I fucked him. "Can I cum inside you?" I asked.

"Not until I cum first," he said, and remained true to his word. I stroked him and fucked him until he was crying out and his sperm started shooting, and every thrust I made sent another gush out of his cock. The feel of his asshole clenching impossibly tighter around my cock made me shoot too, hard. Releasing into him was like sacrilege, or an offering to the gods, either way.

Afterward, when I suggested he stay, I expected him to say no but he stayed and he ate and drank what Henry brought to him before turning in. The next day I asked him, didn't he have to go to work?, and he said he suspected that no, he wouldn't ever really have to work again. He wasn't crazy about the bedroom I'd put him in but he said he'd walk around the mansion later today to try to find one that suited him better, and maybe he'd even take my bedroom if that was the one he liked best.

But that would only happen after he worked out in the gym—nude. Of course I could watch if I wanted, watch him work on the muscle of his beautiful body, which I did.

NEPHILIM LOVER

Rob Wolfsham

I didn't know if Jordan White was just regular Tom Cruise–crazy or if there was some sublime genius to him. I met Jordan in my sophomore year creative writing class. It was an intro class filled with non–English majors forced to take it, so most of them didn't care. But Jordan did. That first day of class, I would never have imagined his incomprehensible, logic-crushing view of reality. If he were just a guy I bumped into in the student union, I simply would have thought of him as some meathead, only interesting because of an impressive bullish physique. His dark brown hair was buzzed close on the sides, a military man's haircut, geometric, structured, like his shoulders and torso. I'd find out later his cleaved musculature was forged from countless hours of obsessive mixed martial arts training. He liked to refer to himself as a Spartan, a facet of his obsession with ancient Greece and their philosophers, an obsession he would eventually want to share with me.

Before the first day of creative writing, the professor made us turn in a story by email so we could get a running start and workshop each other's writing on the first day. Almost everything turned in was horrible or unintentionally funny, mainly because the non-majors didn't care—or didn't understand spell-check. But then again, why even try on the first day when everyone would label you an overachieving asshole?

"Welcome to English Twenty-three Fifty-one, which will hopefully be an exciting escape from your day-to-day rigors," said Dr. Terrell Henderson, our professor, who looked like Teddy Roosevelt with his absurd mustache and rosy cheeks. He sported a Canadian flag pin on the lapel of his tweed coat, an almost too obvious badge of defiance and nonconformity in rural Texas. He sighed through a demure smile and leaned back in his chair, which was in front of his desk so there was no space between him and the surrounding circle in which we slouched. "I want to start by saying I could not be more excited for this class. I was so impressed with the stories you all emailed me. I hope all of you read each other's work and were able to appreciate the artistry and patience you put into your craft."

Really?

"But before we get to your stories, we're going to go around the circle and introduce ourselves, saying our name, major, hometown and one *crazy* fact about ourselves."

This was going to be a long class.

The circle reluctantly shared, wheeling through people who shrugged through the crazy fact with something obviously boring. The third guy to speak was an agricultural science major named Josiah. He wore khaki shorts, a pink Lacoste polo, and a camouflage cap advertising a duck-hunting group. He was from Fort Worth and his crazy fact was that he kept a sawed-off shotgun in his dorm room.

Dr. Henderson laughed nervously, as if a three-year-old had just said *fuck*.

Next was a threateningly beautiful and flighty blonde named Ashley Simpson. Yes, Ashley Simpson. But not the fading pop star Ashlee Simpson. Ashley and Ashlee went to the same Baptist church in Richardson, Texas. And they were friends on Facebook. She giggled through the explanation. She was a human development and family studies major, aka four years of home ec mixed with desperate dating to find matrimonial freedom from collegiate obligation. I envied that.

After a few more forgettable engineering and mass communications majors came the hard-bodied psycho I'd eventually come to know.

"Jordan White," he said flatly to the circle, tilting his head tiredly. He sat with one arm stretched on his desk, one hand on the brim of his silver athletic shorts as he slouched back, knees bouncing in and out, shaved thighs massaging his balls and dick. "I'm from Houston." His eyes narrowed at something on the floor, then he looked up. "I'm interested in dissonance."

The professor did a half nod, half shake. "Could you elaborate?"

Other students perked up at the break in the rhythm of bullshit.

"Yeah," Jordan said. "Dissonance between a priori and a posteriori knowledge. You know, the idea that we're sitting here. I'm supposed to give out a fact. That becomes a posteriori knowledge in your mind about me. But you'll still use preconceptions and understandings about me as a twenty-two-year-old white male to deduce what my thoughts or actions will be in a future event. That's in direct dissonance with what I'm saying."

Fucking philosophy majors. But at the same time, I was floored by the string of word salad that came from the buff meathead.

"I read your story," the professor said, "about the police

officer robbing the convenience store. It was interesting. I look forward to what else you'll be writing for this class." He sighed quickly. "Okay, next." Teddy Roosevelt looked to where I sat. I was three empty seats left of Jordan.

"Um. I'm Greg," I said. "I'm undeclared, from Dallas." I ran a hand through my blond shoulder-length hair.

"Crazy fact?" the professor prompted.

I shrugged. I had a tough act to follow.

Josiah, the guy in the tight pink Lacoste shirt, coughed the word *faggot*. No one seemed to react.

I looked at pink-shirt guy. "My crazy fact is I'm a faggot, but I don't own a pink shirt."

The professor's eyes fluttered in panic, but he smiled. No one really reacted. Either everyone was mentally asleep or they thought I was joking.

Pink-shirt guy blurted, "It's salmon."

"It's gay," I said, icy adrenaline coursing through my stomach. This wasn't the first time I'd called out some jackass I didn't know. I wanted to leap out the window in angry embarrassment—I had wanted to get through this class totally invisible and now that was impossible.

"If everyone would check his or her syllabus," the professor said quietly, "you'll find I won't tolerate any language or writing that attacks someone's race, religion, gender or sexual orientation. I hope that's the only time I have to mention this."

Pink-shirt guy wouldn't look at me, but Jordan White stared at me hawkishly, knees still oscillating in and out, unnerving since I'm used to being the one creepily staring at a guy in class.

We jumped right into workshopping stories. Because I was last to introduce myself—as a faggot—my story was the first one up. It was obvious only two people had read it, since those were the only two who had anything to say.

"I think the story is too sarcastic," Ashley Simpson said to the professor in an unsure way. "The narrator just seems to criticize everyone."

"Hmm, yes," the professor said. "I noticed that too. Do you think that is significant in some way?"

"Um, well, I guess because he's gay?"

I leapt to response. "The narrator is straight."

"Bah, bah, bah!" the professor jumped in. "Cone of silence!" His hands swooped the air around me.

Jordan White raised his hand. "Immanuel Kant's *Critique of Pure Reason* says that your soul is substance and yet simple." He spoke like a soft-voiced preacher. "The homo's story is about the soul connected to the conceptually material. The homo uses the word *I* a lot. That's the soul speaking a noumenon. Perfection within and out. He's God in his realm."

What? I was spellbound by how absurd yet clever he sounded. Some looked at each other. My story was about a nerd getting ready for a party. It sucked. I didn't want to try hard for the first day and be *that guy*. I hadn't even noticed Jordan call me a homo. It was probably because he'd forgotten my name.

"Please, Jordan," the professor said. "Refer to Greg as gay or use the full word *homosexual*. Wait, homosexual? Is homosexual okay?" He looked at me. "Oh, cone of silence, never mind."

For an awkward moment, everyone was in a cone of silence, just the hum of the air conditioners and fluorescent lights around us.

"Let's move on to the next story," the professor said, sighing. "Pass your critiques to Greg." Papers shuffled. I got a stack of copies of my story with written critiques like *Good job* and nothing else; several had nothing written at all; another copy had every semicolon slashed out and replaced with a comma.

I found Jordan White's critique. He'd written a book on top of my story: black ink everywhere, scribbled furiously, entire paragraphs circled, sentences underlined, just an absurd mash of squeezed, nearly microscopic handwriting in the margins and between the double spacing. I could make out bizarre phrases like, "I side with the just man who does unjustly for justness" and "Children of Schem" and then at the very end a simple command to "Read Sitchin to find absolute knowledge."

I would come to know later what that meant.

"How about we move along the circle counterclockwise," Professor Henderson said, looking to Jordan. "Everyone find Jordan White's story and let's get into that."

Only Ashley Simpson and I had anything to say about the story, and we had a brief argument about how Jordan used "too many big words." I countered by saying a dictionary helps, and that despite his story being intimidating I thought it was a sophisticated piece that played with the "justness" of authority figures. In fact, I was being complimentary because I wanted to disagree with Ashley. The story was actually meaningless drivel about a cop robbing a convenience store, an obvious inversion of irony and an obvious polemic against authority.

The professor chastised the rest of the class for not reading. Pink-shirt guy said his email was messed up. Others joined in on that excuse or gave their own.

Jordan's stare burned a hole through my face. He was in the cone of silence, but I wasn't sure if I had flattered or insulted him by missing some grand point.

Class let out early since the professor discovered almost no one had read any of the stories we emailed to each other. He said from now on everyone would just have to pass out his or her story in class for workshopping next time.

Our class was one of the last evening classes in the department. The English building was almost deserted except for us. Mostly everyone took the main stairs and elevator down but I went to grab a Coke from the machine and then entered the east elevator.

I was alone. As the double doors began to close, I heard footsteps stomping closer. The doors were inches apart when a hand lunged through the small opening and grabbed a door and pushed them apart.

"Fuck!" I yelled.

Jordan entered, a backpack slung over one endless shoulder. He stood about six five. He had to have been at least 230 pounds. I caught my breath. "Fuck, you scared me."

Jordan stood facing me as the doors shut behind him. "Did you really mean what you said?"

The slow-as-hell hydraulic elevator began its descent from the sixth floor. "In the critique?"

"Yes, about how the cop in my story was an example of unjust authority."

"Well, yeah, but I wasn't being very profound."

"You were right. Different from the others who spoke," he said.

"Good," I said, unsure how to take that. "You're different from what I expected, that's for sure."

"What did you expect?"

"When I read your story, I expected some pretentious creative writing major with a stupid mustache and a fedora."

He smiled, the first break in his serious shell, a crumpled smile like he wanted to frown or not show his teeth. His angular face grew more attractive with a little humor in it. He said nothing and I felt like I had to fill a gap. "What did you expect when you read my story?"

"A scrawny homosexual."

I nodded. "Oh, okay. Well, you're perceptive. Have you bought the novel we're supposed to read for this class? Pam Houston's *Waltzing the Cat*?"

"Yes. After reading Schopenhauer, reading Pam Houston cannot compare."

"She's not a philosopher," I said, offering the same smile-frown. "It's just a light romance, a coming-of-age novel."

"She writes to impart her simple a posteriori knowledge on her readers—her narrow view of romance, her negativity because no man wants to fuck her."

"Didn't Schopenhauer have a negative view of women?"

"Only a male's intellect clouded by sexual drive could call the stunted, narrow-shouldered, broad-hipped and short-legged sex, the fair sex."

"What?"

"Schopenhauer said that. You haven't read him."

"I've read his Wikipedia article."

"Wikipedia is rarely true objectivity."

The elevator reached the first floor with a ding. Finally. I hadn't realized it, but Jordan had backed me into the corner of the elevator. He towered over me. His pecs were solid armor. His navy blue shirt hugged his nipples in the cold, sterile air of the English building. There wasn't an ounce of body fat on him. He was pure muscle, from his wide neck down to his bulging hairless calves.

I weaseled my way around him. "I have to get back to my dorm."

I didn't see or hear from Jordan until the next week's class. He said almost nothing through everyone's critiques, and then disappeared when class let out. He didn't stare at me like before, and I was oddly disappointed. But a few days later I got a friend request on Facebook. It came with a message that said, *What chapters are we supposed to read in the book?*

I accepted his request and responded and then got an instant message from him that said, *What's the deal?* We discussed what was needed for next class. I then asked him something that had been nagging me.

I read through the critique you wrote on my story, I typed. *The one that was for the first day of class. What does "Read Sitchin" mean?*

Wow man, was the response. *He will be and already IS the most profound thinker of ALL TIME. Greater than Einstein = emc2. Greater than Herman Kahn game theory.*

Why haven't I heard of him? I typed.

The entire Middle East knows about him. About the Nephilim. About Nibiru. The West has been tricked.

That moment, that one little chat, is where Jordan White's rabbit hole opened up and swallowed me. But I penetrated Jordan's mind by choice. I went in because I was physically attracted to him. I was attracted to his muscles. His writing. His vocabulary. His bullshit. But, first, to his muscles.

Come over and I'll show you, was his next message, enticing little words in that little window.

Jordan's place was in the neighborhood next to campus, so I walked from my dorm. It was only a couple of blocks. He lived in the backhouse of a well-manicured, Tudor-style home. It was nine P.M., but there was still some daylight in early September. I walked through the street's back alley to Jordan's house. He answered the door wearing a black wife-beater and shimmering blue athletic shorts. He was sweating from head to sockless Air Jordans, huffing for air. "You came," he said.

"Why wouldn't I?"

"You sounded scared."

I looked him up and down. "I sounded scared through a chat window? You haven't scared me yet."

Jordan's place was a surprisingly large one-room efficiency. It was spotless, everything tidy, especially the hundreds of books on two ceiling-high bookshelves and a computer desk with papers neatly stacked in individual towers. The centerpieces of the room were a giant Bowflex exercise apparatus and a red punching bag hanging from a large steel stand. There was a flat-screen TV, but no couch, just a king-sized memory foam mattress in the corner with blue boxing gloves sitting on top, the only two items not in some kind of order. The punching bag swayed almost imperceptibly. There was nothing on the white plain walls. The room, despite being orderly, smelled faintly of body odor and pot. Of course pot. Not surprising.

Jordan walked to the bookshelf, leaving me in the doorway. I entered and shut the door. He pulled several books from shelves at random and set them in a neat stack on the desk. I watched the muscles in his deltoids and biceps work, gripped by the black cotton of his A-shirt.

"This is Sitchin?" I asked, thumbing through the stack of books. There were titles like *Secrets of the Ancients*, *The 12th Planet*, *The Stairway to Heaven*, and *Genesis Revisted*. "You can't expect me to read all of these."

"Why not?" Jordan said sternly, pausing in his book retrieval.

"Dude, there's like seven fucking books here."

He held up *The 12th Planet*. It looked to be about five hundred pages. "I read this in an hour."

"I don't believe you."

"Learn how to speed-read."

"I don't believe in speed-reading."

Jordan grabbed my backpack off my arm, an aggressive, unexpected move. His hand had snapped out like a serpent. I jerked back. He unzipped the bag rapidly and yanked out my notebook. A few papers went flying. He opened the notebook and pulled out a stapled story.

"Edgar Allan Poe. 'The Fall of the House of Usher.'"

"That's for English Twenty-three-oh-five."

He looked at the first page. After five seconds he turned a page, then another, then another. I laughed halfheartedly at the dumb display.

After a moment of awkward silence on my part and quick page flipping on his, he looked up and launched into an explanation of Roderick Usher's house in minute detail, describing every plot point as if he were a walking, talking set of SparkNotes. I stopped him after a few seconds. "You probably read it before."

"Do you rely so much on empiricism?"

"Yeah. That's how you learn things. Look, forget the story. I believe you."

"Good. Faith. Absolute knowledge. You will learn to rely on that." He handed me *The 12ᵗʰ Planet*. "Read this one first."

I held it. He said nothing, just looked down at me.

"Now?" I asked. "You want me to read it now?"

"Yes." He walked to his Bowflex and sat on it, reclined and started pulling the overhead bar down, lifting weights. "Don't subvocalize words in your mind. Receive them."

I watched, intoxicated by the sight of his hairless underarms and stressed core muscles working and pulling. His veins stood out, spidering down his solid arms. Some people find that unappealing, too organic, but to me it's blood, life, strength. At least a hundred pounds of resistance thrummed behind him. I tore my gaze away from his spectacular body and looked down at the book. This was fucked up. But I found myself sitting on his foam mattress reading the first few pages, glancing up occasionally to watch Jordan work his body as I worked my mind.

But I actually wasn't working my mind. I still subvocalized the words I read, going at my normal pace, but right away I could tell this was a book of quack science and conjecture, some sort of new-agey bullshit about how ancient Sumerians believed there was a giant "12th planet" of the solar system called Nibiru in a vast elliptical 3,600-year orbit. The planet originally created Earth in a great collision with another planet and it was going to eventually return and destroy us. Oh, yeah—and the planet has alien inhabitants called Annunaki, or Nephilim.

"You don't actually believe this, do you?" I asked after a few pages of the intro.

"Yes," he growled as he lifted even more weight. "It's absolute knowledge." He stopped and looked at me, wiping his sweaty brow. "I know for a fact it is your biological and genetic destiny to read these books." He stretched his sculpted arms, pulling one against his chest, then the other.

"This is kind of hard to swallow," I said. "If there was a giant planet out there, NASA would have discovered it."

"Bodes Law says a planet should be between Mars and Jupiter. But instead we have an asteroid belt. Nibiru is why we had Pangea, why we have the moon. Why Uranus is tilted on its side. Why Pluto's orbit is crooked; it used to be a moon of Saturn."

Wow. The rabbit hole just got a little stupid.

"You know what the Sumerians called Pluto?" he continued on the tangent, not bothering to answer my issue with the theory, my point about NASA. "They called it *Gaga*. Like a baby. The Sumerians knew it was tiny. They knew about Pluto before its discovery by *modern man* in nineteen-thirty." He said *modern man* with disgust.

"You mean modern science," I said. "All of what you're saying is conjecture, based on this one Sitchin guy's ideas about Sumerians, his interpretations."

"Sitchin's brother, Amnon Sitchin, works for NASA. He knows these things too, but he'll be in danger if he talks about it."

"So it's a cover up?" I asked, continuing helplessly on whatever tangent Jordan took me on, because I was feeling awkward pressing him on points about his belief system, like telling a 230-pound Baptist that Jesus never walked on water. I was also simply curious where his thought process went, how it moved. It was a ride, sifting through his random trivia and justifications for absurdity.

"Yes," he answered. "The West is being tricked by Nephilim among us, so that they're not ready for the return, so they can be enslaved by Nephilim. The Middle East knows. Saddam Hussein was trying to find the answers in an ancient Sumerian city in southern Iraq, but Nephilim in our government stopped him. We're not ready. But I'll be."

He started lifting again.

Aliens in our government. Awesome. "Is that why you're working out?" I asked incredulously. "To fight these aliens, these Nephilim?"

"They enslaved us once," he said, lifting and heaving. "They made us from the DNA of monkeys. They needed a smart ape to mine the gold in Africa. They need our planet's gold to survive. When they return, they will enslave us again to mine gold. Then we're going to have to escape onto Nibiru before it destroys the Earth. You will train too. Learn to fight with your body, despite its puny size. I will build your muscle."

Suddenly I forgot the string of stupidity in all of this. That last part sounded hot. "Um. Okay."

I'm not sure why I read Sitchin's books. After leaving Jordan's place, I read half of *The 12th Planet* and finished the rest the next day sitting in the library, utterly convinced of its insanity and pseudoscience, convinced of Jordan's insanity. But I went right along to reading the next book in Sitchin's catalog, *The Stairway to Heaven*. That book dwelled on how the Great Pyramid of Giza was built by those Nephilim aliens. Generally it all sounded like a bad treatment of that Kurt Russell movie, *Stargate*.

But still I went to Jordan's house at least twice a week. I was drawn by his way of thinking. I wanted to see how deep the rabbit hole went. I wanted to know the limits of his conviction, how someone so seemingly smart, someone with a mind as muscular as his body, a mind with gifts like speed-reading and a practically autistic memory capacity, could fall prey to such stupid pseudoscience. It became a routine.

And I went to Jordan's house because I wanted to be close to his muscle, while he trained me to box and kick. He had me watch mixed martial arts training videos, with guys like Randy Couture wearing tight shorts and doing kicks and lunges.

My roommate started asking where I was going all the time. Professors noticed I was tired and sore every day. Most of the time during our sessions Jordan took off his shirt, showing the full splendor of his muscular torso, two broad pale pecs, centered with pink nipples above a hard stack of abs leading down to the V-shaped ridge just above the elastic band of his athletic shorts. He would tell me to take off my shirt too, even though I'm just a 120-pound twink.

In between exhausting, rigorous sessions of punching the bag and punishing his Bowflex, Jordan would sit and light a bowl of weed and argue with me about Sitchin and Nephilim. I would smoke with him and try to reiterate my skepticism of so many of the concepts he took as pure reality. Jordan seemed to like that I kept questioning him, challenging him to defend his thoughts and, perhaps, giving him the sense that he was enlightening me.

"Sitchin could be mistranslating the Sumerian texts," I said on a wet day in October.

"People in a posteriori fields of knowledge say that about Sitchin," Jordan said. "They feel threatened because his ideas will eradicate their useless fields."

"Useless fields? Surely you don't mean anthropology or physics or chemistry?"

"Yes," he said. "Evolutionary biology can't explain how we came from one hominid. But Sitchin already knows."

"Sitchin has a theory. An unproven theory."

"Scholars back him up. You've read three of his books now."

"These aren't exactly peer reviewed," I said. "There's a process in science."

"That process is a part of game theory, economic theory. You feel so reliant on that process because those theories guide everything in our country and world and dictate that humans are simple morons who act to fulfill consumption and productivity, to keep the masses blind to true knowledge."

"Sitchin being true knowledge?" I asked.

"Yes. True knowledge. I think you were brought to me. Your intellectual strength stood out to me in class. I knew your mind would be ready for a challenge."

Another tangent, this time to flatter me. Sitchin was self-absorbed supposition. Not knowledge. Not peer reviewed by modern standards. My question couldn't make this gap clear to him. To Jordan, Sitchin was absolute fact, unquestionable, like Agrippa to Dr. Frankenstein, something requiring cultish devotion. "I was thinking you were drawn to me because I'm gay," I said. "But I guess I was way off."

Jordan sat on his Bowflex and wiped his pecs with a towel. He glanced at my body as I lay on his mattress. I wasn't getting buff from all the training, just wiry. "I've been interested in the subject," he said. "I've thought about ants and how the workers never breed. They evolve because the Earth needs something whose energy is devoted entirely to work and thinking, not breeding."

"Is that why the Nephilim made some people gay?"

"Yeah. They made the Greeks especially that way, so they would be thinkers for the masses to be more productive. Plato. Aristotle. Socrates. They sat around and talked all day and were bisexual. Aristotle was gay, though. But the point is, they were the thinkers because they didn't have women around."

"That sounds a little sexist."

"It's an archetype. We were made to be archetypes. Women are meant to bear young. But modern man has clouded these archetypes with game theory and economics. Back in Greece I would have been a warrior. A Spartan. I would have defended my city. You would have lived in that city as a thinker. You would be there with Socrates to share wisdom. You would drink with these men. You would love with these men."

"What about you? You sound like a thinking man. I am sharing theory with you and challenging you. Would I love with you too?"

"Of course. Love between two men sharing knowledge is a high form of love, maybe the highest. Once, this black guy I was selling weed to sucked my dick."

I coughed, exhaling smoke in bursts at the sudden segue. I sat up from lounging on the foam mattress and puffed the pipe again, like a student perking up at something profound Socrates said in his garden.

"I didn't even know he was gay," Jordan continued. "We were smoking blunts and I pulled over to throw out the roach and the guy pulled my shorts down and started sucking me off."

"Wow."

"I blame Libra," he said. "Libra type is so bold, man. Aristotle was Libra, a prissy Libra trying to suck Plato's penis the same way."

"Did you like it?" I asked, voraciously curious, but trying to be completely mellow.

"It disgusted me because he was a stranger. I had shared nothing with him other than a meaningless transaction around weed. I thought about punching his head. But I was about to nut. In like ten seconds. And then I did and he kept sucking. And then I nutted again. Twice. Real fast. Never happened with a female."

"He must have been good."

"It created dissonance in me. It's a man. But I know I'm not gay."

"You don't have to be gay to enjoy a blow job," I said.

"Enlil, a Nephilim, was angry about how sexual man was. It didn't matter to man. He would fuck male, female, animal. They thought to change that, but they made Athens as an experiment to see if it could be stable and they found that the civilization flourished."

"Good to know," I said. "Whatever you feel, I've liked challenging you to see how strong your convictions are."

"I like it, too," Jordan said. He reached for the pipe in my hand. "Let me hit that."

I leaned back on the foam mattress and touched the glass pipe to my lips. "Come hit it."

He slid down from the workout bench, onto the mattress next to me, the foam contouring deeply to his Herculean body. He plucked the pipe from my hand and picked up the lighter at my side and took a hit. I ran my hand along his broad back, fingers sliding around to his chest. I rubbed his pecs and nipples, then down his abs.

He exhaled and stared straight ahead and said nothing. I

didn't need a response. I just wanted to touch him. I had wanted
to touch his body for weeks.

He grabbed my wrist and stopped me. "Now that you have
read of and argued with what I've asked you to explore, what
do you believe?"

I touched his knee with my other hand, testing the terminus
of his athletic shorts drooping on his thighs. "I can't believe one
hundred percent," I said. "No matter what, there will always be
doubt, there will always be argument. That's just how my mind
works, despite all I've read."

"Virgo," he said, grabbing my shoulder. His calloused hand
encased it completely. "Always skeptical."

"If I yielded right away, I wouldn't be a student. I would just
be a mindless pawn."

He set the pipe and lighter aside and pushed me down on the
mattress. "Your mind wants absolute truth," he said. His hazel
eyes darted over me, from my eyes to my neck, chest, hands,
the crotch of my sweatpants. "I'll make you yield," he said. His
head drifted downward, letting his eyes go from mine. He kissed
my stomach, a warm wet touch below my belly button. I seized
up. Jordan's vast empowering form was twice as wide as my
body. He wrapped his hands around my shoulders, pulling me
toward him as he ran his lips and nose along my stomach up to
my concave sternum.

"This body doesn't exist," he said. "My body doesn't exist."

I grasped his back, kneading the musculature around his
shoulder blades.

"I've come to realize the body is just a vibration in three
dimensions," he said. "Even though my body senses three
dimensions, this spark I feel is energy, your desire for the absolute truth I want to share. The body, male or female, doesn't
matter to the mind."

He pulled my sweatpants down with my boxers, stopping for a second, considering the movement, then he pulled down more until my six inches popped out and slapped against my stomach. His head drifted down again and he licked the underside of my cock from the base on up until his lips came around the head, tongue whirling it into his mouth. He tongued under my foreskin, churning around the head, which sent energy through my balls and groin. I squirmed and groaned and scratched the hard biceps that were pressing against my sides.

"Student, what do you want to feel?" he asked. An order.

"Just relax with me. Stop thinking. Rest your mind."

He sighed, caving onto me, resting his face against my chest, as if some great relief had been handed to him. His abs nestled my straining dick and balls. He slid upward, my cock rolling along each muscular bump of his torso. He slid down again, my precum smearing the crevices of his abs. I tugged on the elastic band of his shorts. He pulled them down over his magnificent pale bubble butt, his muscular glutes shifting as he humped gently against me.

I grabbed hold of his ass, sneaking a finger down into the warm tight crack between his cheeks, rubbing the hairless rim of his asshole. He moaned and lifted his head up from my chest, primed for me to kiss his lips. I leaned in but he pushed me back down.

"No," he said sternly. "I will penetrate you like a scholar would his student, not more." He licked one of my nipples and then gnawed on my rib cage, cupping my back. Then he stopped and looked up again. "Turn away from me."

I turned over and presented my twink ass to a muscle god.

"We are in Athens," he said. "You are Aristotle. I am Plato. We are in the bathhouse of the Lyceum."

This was some fucked-up role-playing, but I was there, I was fucking there, practically with an olive wreath on my blond curly hair, transported to another place and time either from pot or from exhaustion under his mental probing or from my vigorous workout routine. I just wanted to feel him now, instead of hear him.

He put a hand on my back between my shoulders, pushing me into the mattress, arcing my ass up to him. His cock pressed against my asshole and popped into me, hot and greased up and wide as fuck. He didn't start slow. Right away his quads slapped my asscheeks, my hard cock responding to his aggressive interior assault by flinging copious strings of precum onto the mattress. Jordan fell forward, nose and lips pushing into the back of my neck, flattening me fully into the foam mattress, fucking me into it. I groaned and drooled. He cupped my throat and gnawed on the back of my neck and gyrated his cock into me, grinding against my ass like a belly dancer, his magnificent abs rolling along my spine.

"You should know, student," he panted into my ear, "that I haven't told you everything yet."

I grunted affirmatively.

"I am part Nephilim. Like Plato. The blood of giants is in me. That is why we'll survive."

His insanity thrilled my body. I should have shoved him off and run out the door, but I couldn't stop this muscular fuck, not for anything.

He stopped his rapid thrusts, holding his dick still in me. He put a palm on my head and pushed my face down into the mattress. He pushed his cock in as far as he could, using just his weight. I wailed in excited terror until his low dangling balls pressed against mine. He wiggled side to side, in me somehow even deeper. It hurt like hell, until his massive dick passed some point inside me where each extra ounce of pressure created individual waves of endless orgasm through my body.

He let up and was upright again and fucked like a bull, sweaty skin slapping mine. He fucked me in near silence and with military precision for several minutes as I groaned and squirmed, my fuckhole more raw and juicy with each slap and slurp. Then he yanked himself out and kneeled over my face, jacking himself off. He grabbed my hair with his free hand, turned my face sideways and pushed the head of his cock into my mouth. I tasted my ass and sweat and musk, and suckled greedily. The first blast of cum splashed against my lips, another stream lanced over my eye into my hair, another splashed across my cheek, then more cum spurted against my tongue and down my face. I slobbered his knob as his jacking slowed, swallowing what essence of him I could. He relaxed and straddled my shoulders, pinning me to the mattress. With my head turned sideways I looked up at him, my face covered in cum. He petted my hair, smearing his spunk into my blond curls. His knuckles rubbed down my cheek, pulling globs of cum to my lips. I licked them from his fingers, then moved to the leftovers on his glistening pink cockhead.

Then he was up, toweling himself off, leaving me nestled in an indentation in the foam mattress. I watched him wipe down his glorious Spartan figure, scooping around his sagging semihard dick and balls.

He said nothing to me as I dressed—then, when I headed for the door, reminded me to read the next Sitchin book before I saw him again.

I panicked, mildly, when Jordan didn't show up to the next class, but he called me later that night and commanded me to come over. We watched a documentary on Sumerian lexicography while he fucked me as if I were a rag doll sitting in his lap. After that, we fucked every time I came over, sometimes after strenuous workouts and serious pot smoking, sometimes after rigorous arguments about science and theology—and serious pot smoking. By the end of the semester, we went at each other almost every day, though he was nonchalant about the fucking. It was seemingly not sexual for him—more like an exchange, two men philosophizing and ruminating on the nature of this planet's dire destiny and then each of us making the other cum. Pretty simple.

I started role-playing a greater interest in his beliefs. I wanted to please him, make him feel like he was making progress with me even though he really wasn't. I still thought he was insane. I thought it was all insane. But by December, I had become so absorbed in his infectious cleverness, his enormous strength, his amazing body—and, most of all, his ability to induce, time after time, addictive full-bodied orgasms—that suddenly I found myself arguing the greatness of Sumerian astronomical calculations, sounding like a chapter in one of Sitchin's books. I wasn't sure if it was just a really bad high from the weed, or if I wasn't really role-playing anymore. But that night, after my apparent impassioned enlightenment, Jordan fucked me with heightened passion and even kissed me for the first time; he did things to my willing, wiry body that transformed every other sexual encounter between us into a warm-up exercise. And then he disappeared for the last two weeks of the semester, two bright icy weeks in December, where every day glistened.

I approached Dr. Henderson on the last day of class and asked if he knew what was going on with Jordan. He had missed the last two classes and it seemed he hadn't turned in his final project, a story that had to be more than twenty pages long.

"I'm surprised you don't know," Dr. Henderson said. "You two seemed like you got close. You were like a team each workshop, skewering everyone's stories."

I shook my head. "I've tried calling him. I've gone to his house, but no one's there."

"He wasn't a student at the university," the professor said after some hesitation. "He withdrew the first week of the semester, but because of some computer glitch he was still on my roster. I appreciated his contributions to our class, however eccentric they were. Not sure why he kept coming, though."

I blinked once, holding my eyelids down an extra second, trying to process the information. "Well, then, where did he go?"

"The reason I found out he wasn't a student is because the police arrested him two weeks ago on outstanding warrants from when he lived in Florida. I'm sure he's locked up down there by now."

My heart plummeted through the building's six floors. I wanted to curl up and shrivel away. Then I wanted to drop-kick a fucking desk out the window, use whatever martial arts skills I had gleaned from Jordan's months of training to hurt something, hurt anything, hurt myself. "What for?" I asked the professor, masking my volcanic rage.

Dr. Henderson's not-quite-handlebar mustache hid the hint of a smirk under rosy cheeks. "No idea. But I'm going to take a wild and crazy guess and say drugs."

The last few class stragglers shuffled out around me. My final project was clenched in my fist, a twenty-five-page story bound in a folder. It was titled *Escape to the 12th Planet,* an encapsulation of how Jordan White saves me from my doomed mundane Earth, my lonely rational world of bitter empiricism and sexual isolation, and suddenly I wished it were all true.

THE GIMP, THE VIG AND THE RING

Michael Bracken

I lifted Jimmy the Gimp by the lapels of his shirt and pushed him back against the brick wall. "You don't have the money," I said, "you know what I got to do."

"Give me a break," the little guy squealed. "I never been late before."

"I need the vig." The vig. The vigorish. The weekly interest due on the money Jimmy had borrowed to bet on a horse that suffered a coronary three strides from the starting gate.

He kicked his good shoe and his corrective shoe with the built-up sole against the brick wall, scuffing the heels. "I ain't got the money, but I can get it."

"How?"

"My momma's engagement ring. I can hock my momma's engagement ring."

"She's not going to like that."

"She won't know nothin'. She's got the Alzheimer's. I'll tell her she lost it."

I liked Jimmy—everybody liked Jimmy—but I had a job to do. I lowered him to the pavement and followed him to the third-floor walk-up he shared with his mother. The hallway outside smelled of curry, cat piss and vomit. I waited while he went inside. I killed time by thinking about Chuck and wondering what he had planned for our dinner. I was relieved when Jimmy slipped out of the apartment a few minutes later and opened his fist to reveal the diamond solitaire his father had given his mother many years earlier.

We walked down the block to Salvatore's and the old man behind the counter gave Jimmy a fair price for the ring. Jimmy shoved the pawnshop ticket in his wallet and the cash in my hands. It was more than enough to cover the week's vig.

"Give it all to Big Tony," he said. "I want to bet the trifecta."

"You sure you want to do that?"

After Jimmy nodded, I folded the stack of Hamiltons in half and slipped them into my inside jacket pocket next to my iPhone. Then we went our separate ways.

I made two more stops that afternoon—at a convent and at a bakery—before I returned to Big Tony's office at the used-book store. I gave my boss all the money I had collected and added a hundred of my own to cover Chuck's vig. I told him what to do with the extra Jimmy the Gimp had given me.

Big Tony separated Jimmy's betting money from the collected vig and pushed it to the side of his desk. "Gimp's already called. Thinks he has inside information on a trifecta."

"You take the bet?"

"Damn right I took the bet."

If my boss had ever had a heart it had long ago turned to stone. Maybe the last decent thing he'd ever done was give me a job when no one else wanted anything to do with me. I'd been a big, dumb jock, just smart enough to play defensive tackle in high school and junior college, but caught with steroids in my possession after a couple of Big Twelve coaches started eyeballing me. Even though I repeatedly tested negative, nobody believed I'd been set up, and I left college without finishing the season or my degree.

Soon after that Big Tony had me running errands. Before long I was collecting his debts. Less than a year later I was wearing custom-tailored suits and had moved from my parents' basement to my own two-bedroom apartment in a rent-controlled building. I went from juco dropout to somebody respected around the neighborhood, all because I became Big Tony's debt collector, and that respect allowed me to live a lifestyle not usually viewed favorably by my business associates.

When I asked if Big Tony had anything else for me, he dismissed me with a wave of his hand.

"I need a new racket," I said as I threw my custom-tailored jacket over the back of the black leather recliner.

Chuck stuck his head out of the kitchen. He'd gotten his hair styled earlier that day, and the stylist had touched up his blond highlights. He asked, "What happened?"

I unclipped my tie and threw it over the jacket. "I shook down a nun with a gambling habit."

Chuck snickered. "What's a nun's gambling habit look like? I'll bet it's black with a white wimple."

"Should you be betting?"

"I guess not." Chastised, my lover ducked back into the kitchen.

I had met Chuck on the job, collecting vig from him on a weekly basis until we each realized what the other kept in his closet, hidden from the rest of the world. We became closer than we should have considering my job and his debt-load, but he had a passion for muscle men—real muscle men, not oiled-up steroid junkies—and I liked a man that didn't mind a few bruises when my lovemaking got rough. Soon enough he moved into my apartment, and I paid Chuck's vig as long as he avoided the ponies and attended Gamblers Anonymous. I realized I'd been snippy with him, so I stepped into the kitchen, leaned down to kiss his cheek, and apologized.

I told him I'd had a rough day.

"Mine was no cakewalk," Chuck said as he continued tossing the salad. Chuck was no small man, but even brushing up against six feet he was still three inches shorter than me and several dozen pounds lighter. He waved one hand toward the kitchen door. "Go. Freshen up. Everything will be on the table in a few minutes."

I had just finished in the bathroom when Chuck called me to the dinner table. He'd made Caesar salad, linguini with clams and garlic butter sauce, and a loaf of garlic bread. He opened a bottle of white wine and poured us each a glass.

Then, over dinner, he told me about his day selling advertising space for a morning newspaper that was hemorrhaging money and threatening layoffs, and I told him about my day collecting Big Tony's debts. I told him about the mechanic who charged customers for work he didn't do just to cover the weekly vig on his off-the-books business loan, about the baker who complained every week about not having enough dough even though the joke hadn't been funny the first time I'd heard it, about the nun who paid the vig on her gambling debts by skimming from the donation plates, and about Jimmy the Gimp.

Everybody knew Jimmy the Gimp was harmless, and Chuck asked, "You didn't hurt him, did you?"

I shook my head. I'd never actually hurt any of the people

whose money I collected, though my size and a persistent, though entirely fictitious, rumor that I'd once used a welsher's head for batting practice certainly put the fear of God into many of them.

"Stealing from his mother is pretty low," Chuck said. "Maybe you should get him into GA. I'll be his sponsor."

"I don't think he's ready," I replied. "He hasn't sunk low enough yet."

Chuck understood how low one had to sink before joining GA. The reason Chuck had moved in with me and had joined Gamblers Anonymous—beyond our mutual attraction—is that he had lost his car and had found all of his things, what hadn't already been picked over by the Dumpster divers and street people, on the curb when he returned home from work one evening. In addition to Chuck, I'd convinced two of Big Tony's other clients to give up the lifestyle, one because he'd fathered a son and the other because his wife needed chemotherapy. Big Tony wasn't pleased with my charity work, but the impact on his bottom line was negligible.

After dinner, Chuck cleared the table and filled the dishwasher while I changed into cross-training shoes, gray sweats, a wife-beater, and black weightlifting gloves. Then he changed into running shoes, shorts, and a pink T-shirt he'd received for participating in a Susan G. Komen Race for the Cure. I grabbed some bottled water and we took the elevator to the basement.

The dank space had been divided into six storage areas that were little more than waist-high walls built of one-by-twos, with chicken wire the rest of the way to the ceiling. The storage spaces weren't secure by any means but half the building's residents each paid an extra two hundred a month just to have use of one of them.

Chuck had helped me convert mine to a workout room,

complete with a weight bench, free weights, exercise mat, tread-mill, heavy bag and a speed bag. He usually accompanied me when I worked out, not because he would be of any help if I dropped the weights, but because seeing me pump iron turned him on and he was always primed to finish the workout in the privacy of our bedroom.

A single bare bulb dangling from the ceiling illuminated our storage area and a small fan in the corner helped circulate the smell of damp basement and sweaty men. We turned both on.

Chuck joined me for stretching exercises. After we limbered up, he jogged on the treadmill while I worked with the free weights. I'm not a bodybuilder. I have no interest in building show muscle, oiling up, and posing near naked before a theater full of Charles Atlas wannabes, horny groupies of all genders and steroid pushers. I maintain my size and strength for my job, relying on my imposing physique more than anything else to intimidate.

My workouts consisted of heavy days and light days, and that night was a heavy day. I put 300 pounds on the barbell and bench-pressed three sets of five reps; squatted three sets of five reps with 400 pounds on the barbell; power cleaned five sets of 250 pounds; and finished with ten 100-pound curls for each arm. My wife-beater was soaked with sweat but I was barely breathing heavy when I finished with the weights.

After draining one of the bottled waters without a pause, I pulled on twelve-ounce boxing gloves and worked the speed bag with a steady *rat-a-tat-tat*. When Chuck finished his jog, I switched to the heavy bag, and he leaned into it while I pummeled it from the opposite side.

I should have been concentrating on my fists and how they landed against the bag because someday I was actually going to get into a fight, but I kept sneaking peeks at my lover. His blue eyes were half closed and his partially erect cock tented the front of his shorts. Because I was paying too much attention to Chuck's package, a roundhouse punch missed the bag and caught him in the upper arm.

Chuck's eyes snapped open and he stumbled backward, releasing his hold on the heavy bag as he went. The bag swung forward and smacked into me with no noticeable effect. I asked, "You okay?"

"Sure," he said as he rubbed his arm.

I peeled off my gloves, hooked one hand behind his head, and pulled him close. I covered his mouth with mine and gave him a deep, tongue-tangling kiss. When it ended, I said, "Let's go upstairs."

One of the first things I'd done after moving into the apartment was remodel the bathroom, tearing out the claw-foot bathtub and replacing it with a custom-built shower appropriate for a man my size—a man my size who liked company. Chuck and I stripped off our sweaty workout clothes, shoved them into the wicker hamper, and slipped into the shower.

He grabbed the bath mitt first, lathered it up with lavender-scented antibacterial body wash and began scrubbing my back and my chest. He worked his way down my body until he was kneeling on the tile floor in front of me, the warm water cascading over us from two separate showerheads and my erect cock bobbing in front of his face.

He used the bath mitt to scrub my heavy ball sac as he leaned forward and took the head of my cock into his mouth. He hooked his teeth behind the spongy soft glans and then bathed my cockhead with his tongue.

I reached down and took his head in my hands, holding it as I pushed my cock deep into his oral cavity. He accepted every inch—something no other man I'd been with had been able to do—before I pulled back and pressed forward again. I moved my hips slowly at first, and then with increasing speed. Soon my ball sac was slapping against Chuck's chin and it slowly tightened up the closer I was to orgasm.

When I finally came, I came hard, firing a thick wad of hot spunk against the back of Chuck's throat. He swallowed every drop and then licked my cock clean before I pulled him to his feet. The workout had turned me on, too, and even though I'd just come my cock only softened for a moment.

I spun Chuck around so that he was facing the tiled wall. We don't keep any lube in the shower, so I grabbed antibacterial soap and dribbled it down his asscrack. He bent forward, shoving his ass back toward me and I pressed my cockhead against his soapy sphincter. Then I grabbed his hips and pressed forward, driving my cock into him.

Chuck braced himself against the tile wall with one hand and wrapped the fingers of his free hand around his erect cock, matching his fist pumps to my rhythm. I came first, slamming into him and holding his hips so tight I bruised them for the second time that month. Then he came, spewing spunk on the tile wall that was quickly washed away by the cascading water.

We finished our shower a bit more sedately than we began it, wrapping matching terry-cloth bathrobes around ourselves and then sitting in the living room and finishing the bottle of wine Chuck had opened at dinner.

When we finally went to bed I fell asleep with my arms wrapped around Chuck, holding him tight as if I was afraid he would escape during the night, knowing that everything was right with the world when I had him in my arms.

I woke up alone: Chuck had already gone for the day when I finally pushed myself out of bed and into the shower. He'd left half a pot of coffee made from freshly ground beans and I downed it before I dressed in a crisply pressed white shirt, clip-on tie and a suit that Chuck had picked up at the dry cleaner's on his way home the previous day. Then I checked my iPhone, saw that I had no messages and made my way to the first pickup of the day.

Time disappeared quickly. I was thinking of lunch at the Pasta Barn, having already collected the weekly vig from four of Big Tony's regulars, when my iPhone rang. I dug in my jacket pocket for it.

As soon as I answered, Big Tony shouted in my ear, "The son-of-a-bitch hit the trifecta and just walked out of here with ten Gs."

"Who?"

"Jimmy the Gimp, that's who."

"You let him leave with all that money?"

"What was I supposed to do?" Big Tony yelled. "I got a reputation. I pay my debts just like I expect people to pay theirs. That's what Jimmy did. I got my cut and then he gimped out of here with 10 Gs of my money."

"What do you want me to do about it?"

"Find the son-of-a-bitch and convince him to lay off some of that money."

After Big Tony disconnected the call, I slid the iPhone back into my jacket pocket alongside two thousand dollars I'd already collected. Instead of visiting the bartender with a hard-on for sports betting, I changed direction and headed back toward Jimmy the Gimp's neighborhood.

I found him by accident when I heard someone shouting as I walked past the mouth of an alley two blocks from Salvatore's. When I turned and entered the alley, I found three guys putting the squeeze on Jimmy behind a foul-smelling Dumpster. The little guy tried to give as good as he got—his heavy corrective shoe connected with one guy's nut sac and drove him to his knees—but he was outnumbered and one of the guys held a length of pipe that he was using to play stickball with Jimmy's noggin.

Before I could reach them, Jimmy was on the ground, curled in a ball, and he'd stopped resisting. One of the three punks tore Jimmy's jacket off of him.

I grabbed the nearest guy and slammed his head against the recently emptied Dumpster. The Dumpster clanged like a church bell and the punk dropped to his knees. I swung at the next guy, missing with a roundhouse left when he stepped inside of it. He grabbed my tie and brought his knee up toward my groin, but my clip-on tie came off in his hand and he lost his balance. A right uppercut to his chin sent him to the ground with his pal, leaving only the guy with the pipe to deal with.

He took one look up at me, dropped the pipe and ran with Jimmy's jacket still gripped tightly in one hand. His two buddies scrambled to their feet and followed. I thought about giving chase but figured they could outrun me. I spent too much time in weight training and, despite Chuck's encouragement, not enough time doing cardio.

I knew Big Tony would put word out on the street and that by the end of the week we'd know the names of three punks flashing wads of cash they had no logical right to, so I turned my attention to Jimmy the Gimp.

He hadn't moved.

I sat beside him, not concerned about the filth staining the seat of my suit pants, and cradled the Gimp's head in my lap.

"The ring," he said, slurring his words. Blood trickled from his ear. "I was going to get my momma's ring."

That was the last thing Jimmy the Gimp said before he closed his eyes forever. I took the pawnshop ticket from his wallet and retrieved his mother's engagement ring from Salvatore's, using my own money because the three punks had gotten away with Jimmy's winnings.

Then I walked down the block and up two flights of stairs. The hallway outside the Gimp's apartment still smelled of curry, cat piss and vomit, and I tapped lightly on the apartment door.

A moment later a weathered old woman wearing mismatched shoes and a faded blue housedress that hadn't been properly fastened jerked the door open and stared up at me. "Do I know you?"

"No, ma'am," I said, "but I knew Jimmy." I handed her the engagement ring. "He said you lost this."

After she took the ring from my hand and put it on her finger, I turned and walked away. The police would come soon enough to tell her what had happened to her son.

I needed Chuck. I needed him to hold me and tell me everything was going to be okay. I pulled out my iPhone and dialed his number.

BIGCHEST: CONFESSIONS OF A TIT MAN

Larry Duplechan

I'm pretty sure it all started with Steve Reeves. For the benefit of people younger than myself (and lately, that seems to include just about everybody), Steve Reeves was sort of the Arnold Schwarzenegger of the 1950s and '60s—only back in those days, success in professional bodybuilding *could* be parlayed into a career in action/adventure movies but *not* into the governorship of California. By 1950, Reeves had won all of the major bodybuilding contests then in existence (well, both of them: it was Mr. America, Mr. Universe, and that was it). In the early '50s, he appeared as sort of beefcake window dressing in a couple of biggish Hollywood movies (I seem to recall seeing him lifting Jane Powell with one hand); and in 1958 he sojourned to Italy where he starred in the title role of *Hercules*. The sequel, *Hercules Unchained*, followed in 1959.

By the late 1960s, by which time I was a boy on the cusp of my teen years, both of Steve Reeves's *Hercules* movies (in addition to his other post-*Hercules* flicks such as *Romulus and*

Remus and *The Last Days of Pompeii*—all of them Italian-made sword-and-sandal epics so, well, Herculean, that I still think of them as "*Hercules* movies") were staples of afternoon and late-night television, at least in the greater Los Angeles area. Back in the day, KCOP-Channel 9's "Million Dollar Movie" showed the same movie every day at 4:00 P.M. for five consecutive days, Monday through Friday—which is why I can still recite *The Pajama Game* (Doris Day and John Raitt) nearly word-for-word, song-for-song; and why *Hercules* starring Steve Reeves is etched upon my brain as indelibly as the Pledge of Allegiance.

As with any beautiful thing, words cannot do justice to the beauty of Steve Reeves in his heyday. He was square-jawed and boyishly handsome (even with the close-cropped beard he wore in his Hercules movies), with a head of thick, wavy dark hair. At just over six feet tall and weighing 215 pounds, Reeves sported one version of the perfect physique: a twenty-nine-inch waist, manta-ray lats flaring up to impossibly wide shoulders, and a fifty-two-inch chest. That's right—a fifty-two-inch chest. As a boy, I found that chest absolutely fascinating; not only the super-human breadth and depth of Reeves's rib cage, but especially the twin mounds of chest muscle for which I had, at that time, no proper name. They bulged when Steve crossed his massive arms and bounced heavily when he ran. I don't know if I or my brother Lloyd (two and a half years younger than myself, and a *Hercules* fan himself—though not in quite the same way I was), first coined the term, but at some point we began referring to Steve Reeves's impressive set of chest muscles as "bigchest" (one word, accent on the first syllable). As in, "Wow, did you see his *big*chest move when he killed that hydra?"

By that point (the age of eleven or twelve), I knew, and on some level accepted the fact, that I liked to look at other boys and good-looking, athletic grown men. *Hercules* taught me that I really liked men with big muscles, and that I especially liked men with bigchest. But it was an episode of "Bewitched" that taught me the correct term for what I liked so much. All I remember of the scene itself was that there was a female client at the ad agency where Darrin Stevens worked and for some reason there was a line-up of competitive-size bodybuilders in posing trunks being presented to this client. My prepubescent crotch swelled to aching as the musclemen posed and flexed, until finally they all began making their chest muscles bounce up and down. The lady client asked, "How do they make those things *pop* like that?" Someone (maybe Darrin, maybe Larry Tate, maybe someone else), answered, "Those 'things' are called *pecs*."

Pecs. I liked pecs. And I really liked seeing them bounce. On some variety show at about the same time, I remember seeing a bodybuilder make his pecs bounce rhythmically (right-left-right-left) while whistling "shave-and-a-haircut, two-bits," which nearly shorted out my circuits, and left me with a fairly vibrating hard-on I had no idea what to do with (I wouldn't discover masturbation for another couple of years).

Back in the day (and we're talking the mid- to late 1960s here), television wasn't the smorgasbord of shirtless hunks that it is nowadays (and I'm not even counting premium cable channels—on the CW, it's a relative rarity to see a young man with his shirt *on*). It wasn't that you never saw men with their shirts off—this was the era of the *Beach Party* movies—it's just that most actors weren't particularly buff in those days. Everybody seemed to know *How to Stuff a Wild Bikini*, but America wasn't nearly so concerned with the proper stuffing of the wild tank top. Sightings of a really good set of pecs on the tube were few and far between when I was a chest-crazy kid, but I still remember some of them, fortysomething years later. Johnny Weissmuller's pecs were overripe even in his first film appearances in the late 1930s,

200   MUSCLE MEN

and over the twenty-odd years of his career as star of MGM's
series of *Tarzan* movies (Saturday afternoon movie staples), they
grew increasingly pendulous. I minded not a whit. Gordon Scott
was another massive-but-not-lean Tarzan, and something of a
male Jane Russell, chestwise: a full-figured guy. Former foot-
baller Mike Henry was the first truly ripped Tarzan, and his
pecs seemed to have been chiseled from solid granite. Needless
to say, if a *Hercules* movie wasn't on tap, a *Tarzan* movie would
do me just fine.

When Peter Lupus (pre–"Mission Impossible") showed off
his Mr. America physique to Annette Funicello in *Muscle Beach
Party*—inviting her to "Look at that tricep. See how I can make
it ripple?"—I was staring not at the rippling of Peter's truly
impressive upper arm, but at the way the pec nearest that arm
bunched and bulged as he flexed. While he was no muscle god,
Alejandro Rey (Carlos Ramirez in "The Flying Nun," one of
my favorite shows at the time—hey, I was just a kid) sported a
set of lean, muscle-striated pecs in his all-too-infrequent shirtless shots. Even the relatively mature Eddie Albert appeared
sans shirt at least once on "Green Acres" (wearing only pajama
bottoms, if memory serves), showing a more-than-respectable
set of pecs, especially for a man his age—though his chest was
so hairy his pelt obscured his nipples completely. I vividly recall
my kid brother commenting, "He has no *dots!*"

If I had to wait for the occasional glance at shirtless man-
tits on TV, the good news was that growing up in Southern
California afforded me a view of plenty of well-muscled shirtless boys and men, "live" and up close. As it happened, the
onslaught of puberty (and the unrequited longings and incon-
venient erections that went with it), coincided with a two-year
stay in Sacramento, where we were the only black family in
the neighborhood, and where the long, hot summers meant

the neighborhood boys spent most of their non-school time with their shirts off. And much as I hated mandatory P.E. in school, it had the desirable side effect that even the least athletically inclined boys were usually in pretty good physical condition. And boys who played sports or lifted a dumbbell now and again were like walking porno. I remember with particular fondness the Meyers brothers from down the street: Greg, Andy and Jeff—handsome, tousle-haired, touch-football-on-the-front-lawn-playing boys with near-identical hairless, sculpted chests that I found mouthwatering, individually or as a trio. There was Roy Jarrett, who kept me hiding my boner behind my books my sophomore year in high school. Hazel-eyed with close-cropped, curly, honey-colored hair, Roy was so beautiful I made believe I was interested in becoming a Jehovah's Witness just so I could watch his lips as he read aloud from his green-bound Bible. Seeing Roy's perfect pecs in the boys' locker room, fresh from the showers, droplets of water falling from his perky nipples, was a religious experience such as neither Roy's Kingdom Hall nor my Baptist church could afford me.

Mr. Shell, our next-door neighbor (and the father of a couple of the kids I palled around with), was as unlikely as his sons to be seen after working hours wearing a shirt. Mr. Shell's pecs were reminiscent of Johnny Weissmuller's—just a shout away from man-boobs—and sat atop something of a beer belly. But as with the early Tarzan, I cared not a whit. I thrilled to the sight of those meaty pecs bouncing, quite independent of each other, as Mr. Shell ran toward me during one of the frequent games of kick-the-can he organized with the neighborhood kids. As with heterosexual tit-men and the female breast, I don't really have a working concept of "too big" when it comes to the male chest. And besides, Mr. Shell was good looking, considerably more fun than my own father (no slouch in the pecs department himself, but he wouldn't have been talked into playing in the street with a bunch of kids at the point of a gun), and in addition to his somewhat gone-to-seed bigchest, Mr. Shell also had beautiful feet (but that's another fetish).

Then there was Dick Beeson, my P.E. teacher during junior year in high school. Coach Beeson was handsome enough and buff enough to have starred as either Hercules or Tarzan (he made TV-Tarzan Ron Ely look like a flagpole by comparison). Underneath his polo shirt, Coach Beeson's pecs formed a high-set mantle of muscle you could have set football trophies on. The one time I saw him without that shirt (emerging from his office to quell some sort of locker-room shenanigans, wearing only his gym shorts, not only magnificently bare-chested but—bonus!—barefoot), I'm pretty sure I made a noise and my hands were just barely fast enough to cover my instantaneous erection with a towel. It was while replaying that scene in my testosterone-poisoned little teenaged brain, humping my sheets as quietly as I could so as not to awaken my brother in the twin bed across the room, that I had my first orgasm, hosing down at least half my mattress with what I remember as an inordinate volume of yeasty-smelling boy cum. Following a brief spasm of fear that I might have somehow shot blood and might die of my self-inflicted wound, I spent the next several years' worth of spare moments doing little other than masturbating, often while thinking about Coach Beeson.

My desire for Coach Beeson (his feet and face, thighs and ass, biceps, triceps and especially pecs) was accompanied by the newfound desire to have pecs of my own. I started lifting weights, grunting out set after set of bench presses on the school's Olympic weight machine like a boy possessed, my eyes quite literally on the prize: when I wasn't actually staring at Coach

Beeson's awesome rack, I was visualizing it. And as very often happens when one is truly focused, I achieved my goal.

It only took about twenty years.

See, I was a late bloomer. I sang soprano until I was nearly fifteen, and didn't reach my adult height (all of five foot eight) until I was seventeen and entering college. Even then, I was every ounce of 125 pounds. So even though all that weight training made me unexpectedly strong for my size (I was a surprisingly good arm wrestler, known for taking down boys outweighing me by twenty or thirty pounds), I just couldn't seem to get big. All my efforts to the contrary, I remained so slender that by my freshman year in college, I found I was often mistaken for a woman. Daily, even. In a T-shirt, Levi's and sneakers, I was addressed, "Excuse me, Miss," by strangers and was constantly hit on by lesbians. I'd come home, seething, to my then-boyfriend (now my husband), Greg, who quipped, "Whip out your dick. That'll show 'em." (By the way: while I can truthfully say I married for love, it does not hurt matters that my husband has a dynamite set of pecs.) There were no public whippings-out of my dick. Instead, I worked out all the harder. And in time, I finally began to see results—in my arms. And while my chest development continued to disappoint, my new biceps/triceps combo (and the tight T-shirts I wore to display them) succeeded in rendering me considerably less equivocal, genderwise.

I was in my midthirties—countless bench presses, dumbbell flies, cable crossovers and protein shakes later—when a cute young gay dude (recently hired in the word processing department where I also toiled), sidled up to me, a flirtatious twinkle in his eye, and said, "Dude, you lift *trucks* or something?" By that point, I had grown used to a certain number of compliments on the size of my arms. "Small Japanese trucks, mostly," I replied. "Why do you ask?" The cutie responded, "Big chest."

Yes! To paraphrase Jean Hagen in *Singin' in the Rain,* all my hard work had not been in vain for nothin'. I wasn't sure when exactly it had happened, but I had apparently, finally, achieved my goal: bigchest was mine. That little exchange with the word processing muffin was sufficiently significant for me that I fictionalized it in my third novel.

So in case you're ever in the mood to flatter me regarding my physique, keep in mind that my father has great arms, and his father had great arms, so if any body part was going to develop, it was going to be my arms. And since I'm still a big fan of snug-fitting T-shirts, arms are what most people tend to notice first. But relatively speaking, arms were easy. Chest was tough. Compliment my pecs, and you're sure to get a smile out of me. Hey, I might even bounce 'em for ya.

ABOUT THE AUTHORS

JONATHAN ASCHE has been writing for more than fifteen years, appearing in *Friction 3*, *Best Gay Erotica 2004, 2005* and *2007*, and *Hot Gay Erotica*. He is the author of two novels, with a story collection, *Kept Men and Other Erotic Stories*, due in 2011. He lives in Atlanta with his husband, Tomé.

STEVEN BEREZNAI (stevenbereznai.com) is the author of the gay teen superhero novel *Queeroes* and the how-to book *Gay and Single...Forever? 10 things every gay guy looking for love (and not finding it) needs to know.*

MICHAEL BRACKEN's short fiction has been published or is forthcoming in *Best Gay Romance 2010*, *Boys Getting Ahead*, *Country Boys*, *Flesh & Blood: Guilty as Sin*, *Freshmen*, *Hot Blood: Strange Bedfellows*, *The Mammoth Book of Best New Erotica 4*, *Men*, *Ultimate Gay Erotica 2006* and many other anthologies and periodicals.

YANN DUMINIL trained as an illustrator at the Emile Cohl Drawing School in Lyon, France, earning a degree in illustration and comics. He now lives near Paris with his boyfriend. *NIGHTLIFE* is his first published work as a comics colorist.

LARRY DUPLECHAN is the author of five gay-themed novels, including *Blackbird* and the Lambda Literary Award–winning *Got 'Til It's Gone*. He lives in Woodland Hills (a suburb of Los Angeles) with his lawfully wedded husband and their Chartreux cat, Mr. Blue.

JAMIE FREEMAN (nickdreamsong.blogspot.com) lives in Gainesville, Florida—the heart of the Gator Nation. He's not much for football, but he's a huge Dolly Parton fan. His short stories have appeared in a wide range of anthologies. Email him at jamiefreeman2@gmail.com.

JACK FRITSCHER (jackfritscher.com) introduced muscle sex into gay literature in his best-selling 1969 novel *Leather Blues*, perfecting that genre as founding editor of *Drummer*, and authored the definitive muscle-worship novel *Some Dance to Remember*. Lammy finalist Fritscher joined his first gym at sixteen in 1955, started photograping bodybuilders in 1961, and founded Palm Drive Video (1984-1999).

THOMAS FUCHS has spent much of his career writing television documentaries and some nonfiction. Over the past few years, he has discovered the joy of imagining and inventing afforded by the writing of fiction. He can be reached at fuchsfoxxx@cs.com.

JEFF JACKLIN (jeffsmusclestudio.com), a lifelong artist, started weight lifting at twenty-one, has competed in power-lifting meets, and has studied Tae Kwon Do and Kung Fu—all real-life experience he brings to his muscle art, which includes four volumes of *Hearts & Iron™*, about two iron-pumping gay lovers.

BASTIAN JONSSON (boytoygraphics.com), born in 1973, is a self-taught comic artist, illustrator and graphic designer, a lifelong comics addict and aspiring creator. He lives in rural west Sweden with his long-suffering veterinary boyfriend. His art appears in *Stripped: Uncensored*; *NIGHTLIFE*, written by Dale Lazarov, is his first book-length work of comics.

GEOFFREY KNIGHT (geoffreyknight.blogspot.com) is the author of the hit gay adventure series *Fathom's Five*, which includes *The Cross of Sins*, *The Riddle of the Sands* and *The Curse of the Dragon*. Geoffrey is a lover of handsome heroes, evil villains and tall tales. He lives in Sydney.

DALE LAZAROV (dalelazarov.tumblr.com) is the writer/editor of gay erotic comics such as *STICKY* (drawn by Steve MacIsaac), *MANLY* (drawn by Amy Colburn), and *NIGHTLIFE* (drawn by Bastian Jonsson), all published by Bruno Gmünder Verlag. He's currently collaborating on several new gay erotic comics projects and lives in Chicago.

JOE MAROHL (kublakong.blogspot.com) holds a doctorate in seventeenth-century British literature, teaches writing and literature at a community college in North Carolina, and publishes a wrestling kink blog, Ringside at Skull Island.

CAGE THUNDER (myspace.com/cagethunder) is a wrestler for BGEast.com, and the pseudonym of a New Orleans mystery writer. He has published stories in *Rough Trade, How the West*

Was Done and *Tented*. A collection of his wrestling stories, *Going Down for the Count*, is forthcoming. Friend him on Facebook.

NATTY SOLTESZ (nattysoltesz.com) has recently been published in *Best Gay Erotica 2010* and *Best Gay Romance 2010*. He cowrote the 2009 porn film *Dad Takes a Fishing Trip* with director Joe Gage, and is a faithful contributor to the Nifty Erotic Stories Archive. He lives in Pittsburgh with his lover.

ROB WOLFSHAM (wolfshammy.com) is nearing a quarter-life crisis and hopes you jacked off to his story because he needs validation. His work has appeared in several anthologies, including *Best Gay Erotica 2010* and *College Boys*. He is trapped in Lubbock, Texas.

ABOUT
THE EDITOR

RICHARD LABONTÉ was a gay bookseller for twenty years, has written gay book reviews for more than thirty years, and has edited about thirty (mostly erotic) gay anthologies for Cleis Press and Arsenal Pulp Press. He lives a quiet gay life on Bowen Island, a short ferry ride from Vancouver, with his gay husband, Asa Dean Liles, and their two dogs, who often act gay, though they are, respectively, neutered and spayed. Several editions of the *Best Gay Erotica* series, which he has edited since 1996, have been Lambda Literary Award finalists, and two have won, as has *First Person Queer* (Arsenal Pulp), coedited with Lawrence Schimel.